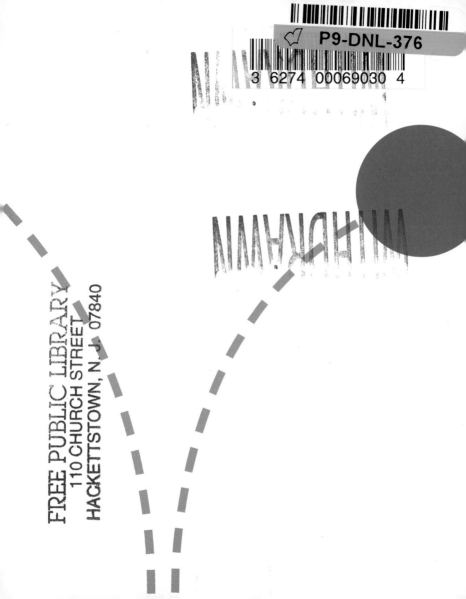

P9-DNL-376

3 6274 00069030 4

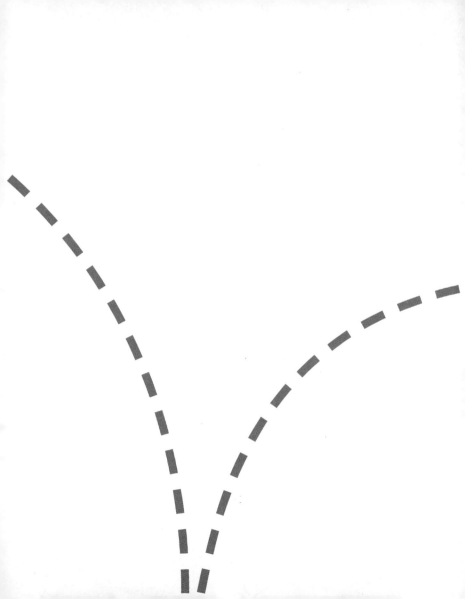

THE DOT &

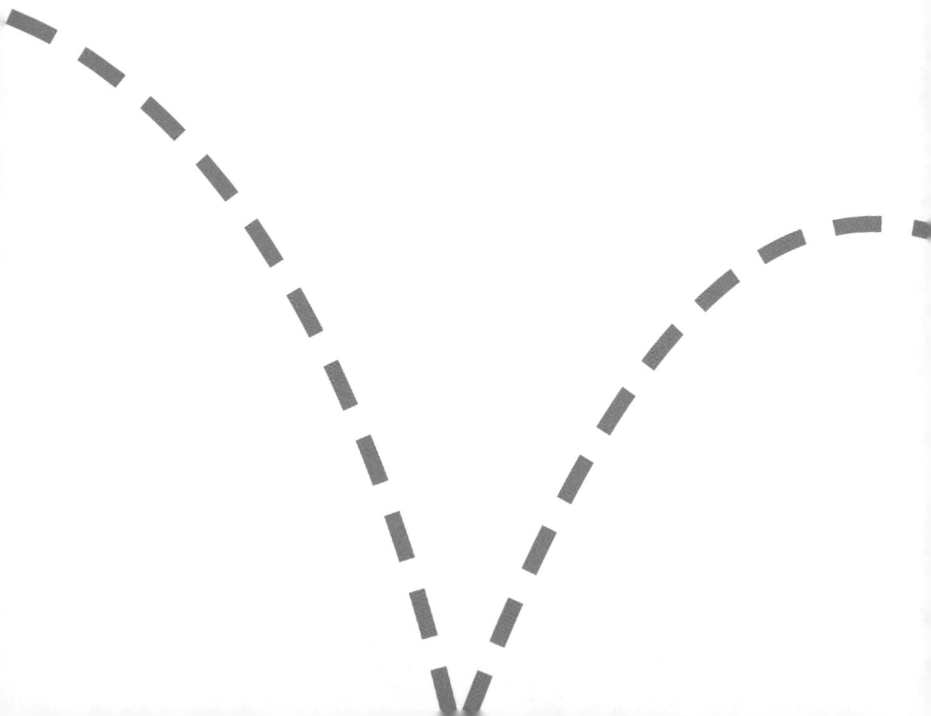

THE LINE

a romance in lower mathematics

NORTON JUSTER

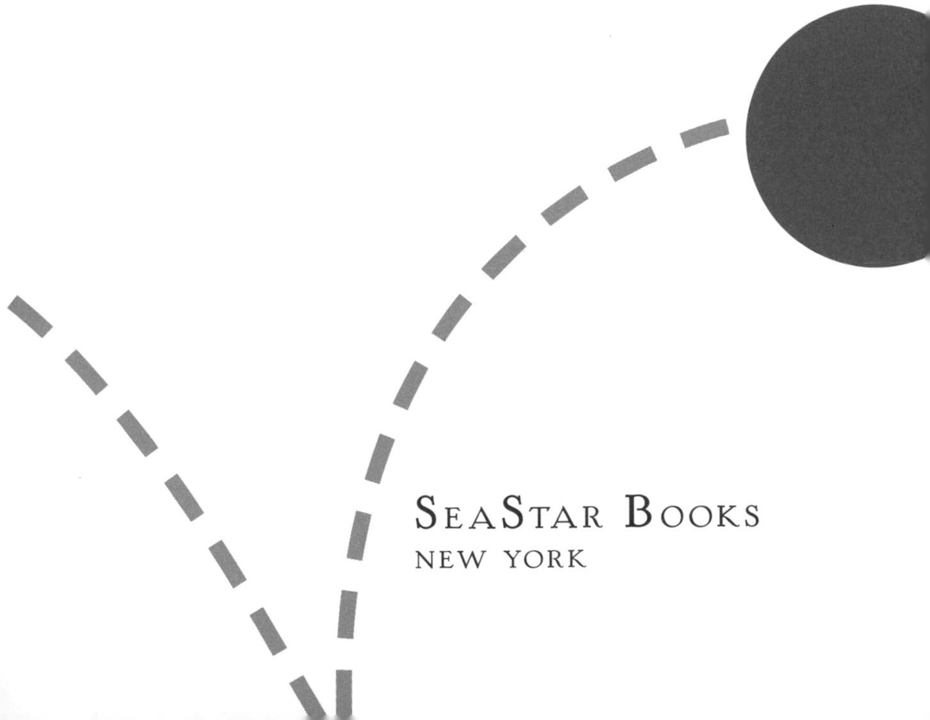

SEASTAR BOOKS
NEW YORK

Acknowledgments
The American Museum of Natural History: Spiderweb; Bettmann/Corbis: Euclid, Tug of War, Tightrope Act (Wallendas), New York Street Scene; ArtResource/Alinari: Charles V on Horseback *by Titian; George Paul Schmidt: Cupid illustration; Scripta Mathematica: pictures for "Complex," "Enigmatic," and "Compelling"; George Wittenborn, Inc.: picture for "Clever," inspired by* Little Jester in a Trance, *from* The Thinking Eye *by Paul Klee, The Documents of Modern Art Series, Vol. 15, published by George Wittenborn, Inc., 1961*

First published by Random House, Inc., New York, 1963.

SEASTAR BOOKS
A division of NORTH-SOUTH BOOKS, INC.

Published in the United States by SeaStar Books, a division of North-South Books, Inc., New York. Published simultaneously in Canada by North-South Books, an imprint of Nord-Süd Verlag AG, Gossau Zürich, Switzerland.

Library of Congress Cataloging-in-Publication Data is available.
The text for this book is set in 14-point Colwell.

ISBN 1-58717-066-3
TB 10 9 8 7 6 5 4 3 2 1

Printed in the United States of America

For more information about our books, and the authors and artists who create them, visit our web site: www.northsouth.com

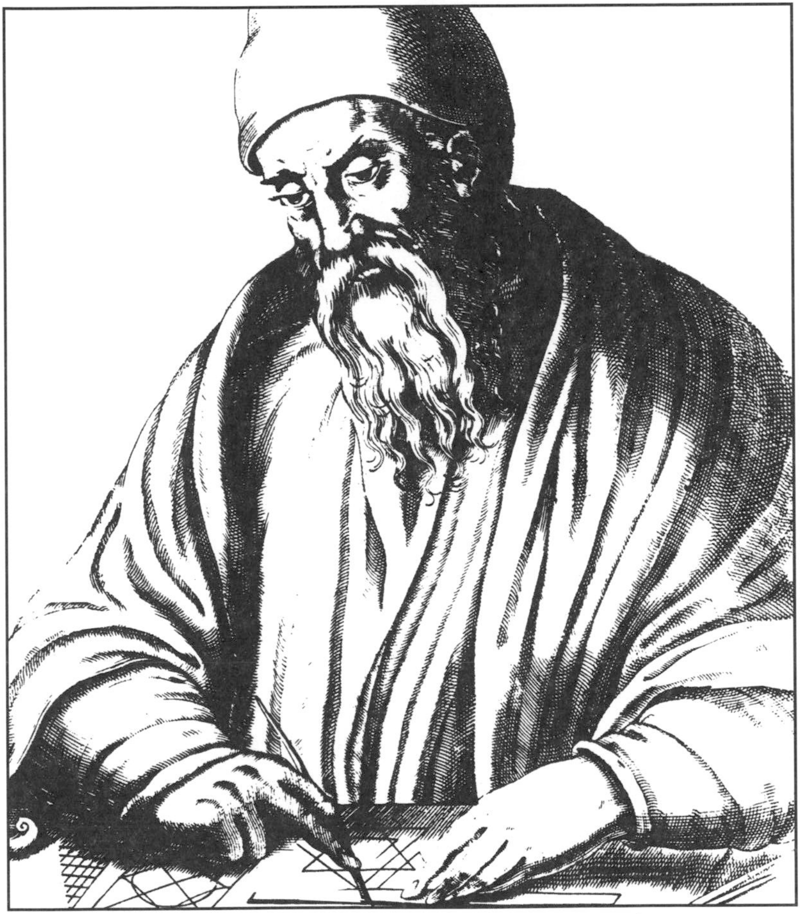

For Euclid, no matter what they say.

*O*nce upon a time there was a sensible straight line

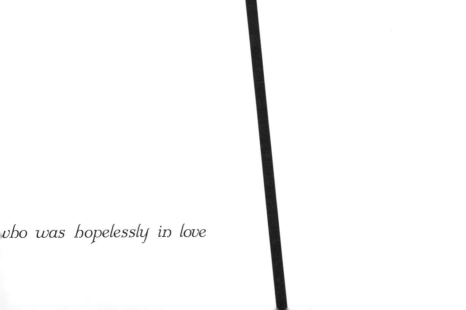

who was hopelessly in love

with a dot.

"You're the beginning and the end, the hub,
the core and the quintessence," he told her tenderly,
but the frivolous dot wasn't a bit interested,

for she only had eyes for a wild and unkempt squiggle who never seemed to have anything on his mind at all.

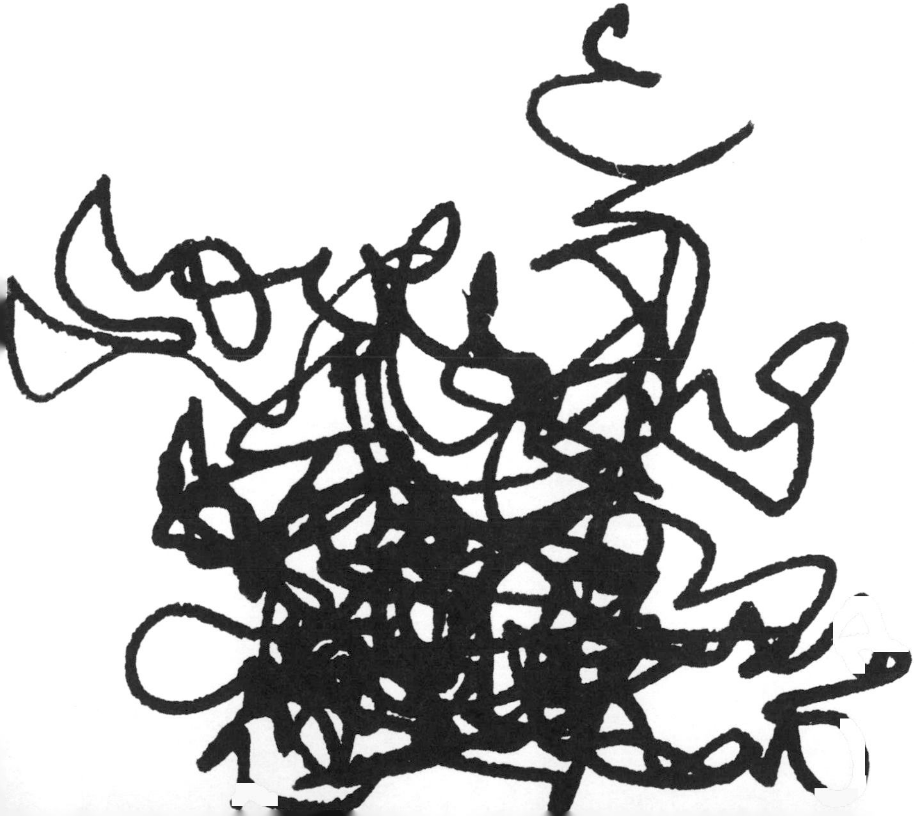

They were everywhere together,
singing and dancing and frolicking
and laughing and laughing
and lord knows what else.
"He is so gay and free,
so uninhibited and full of joy,"
she informed the line coolly,

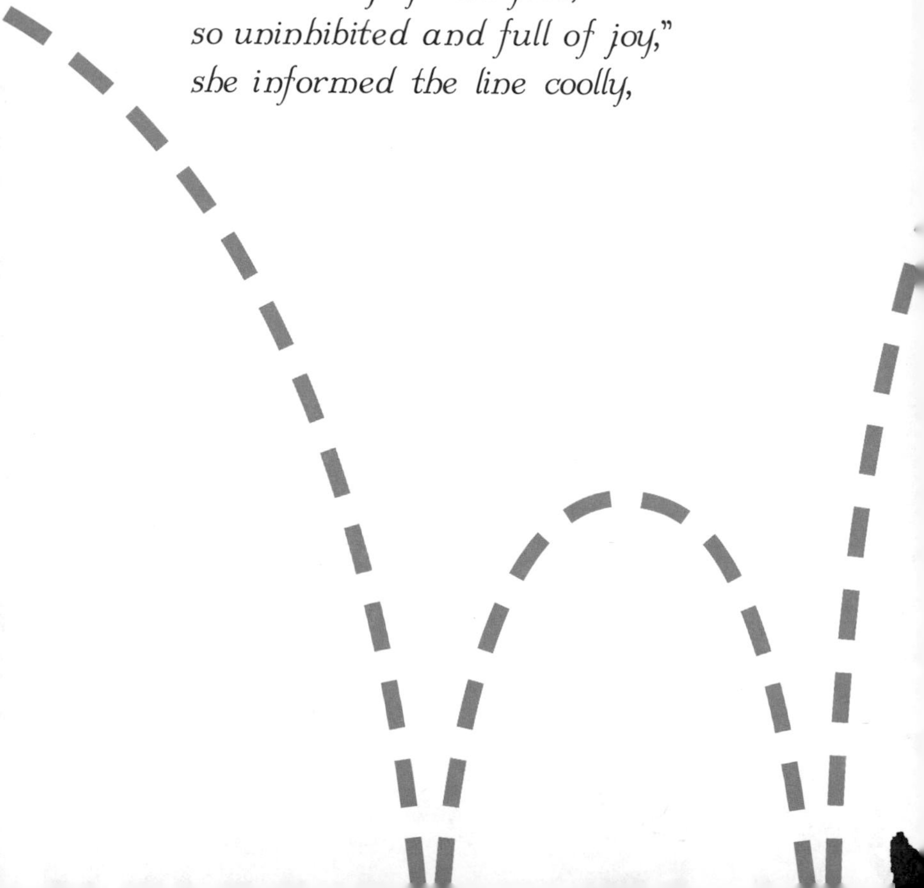

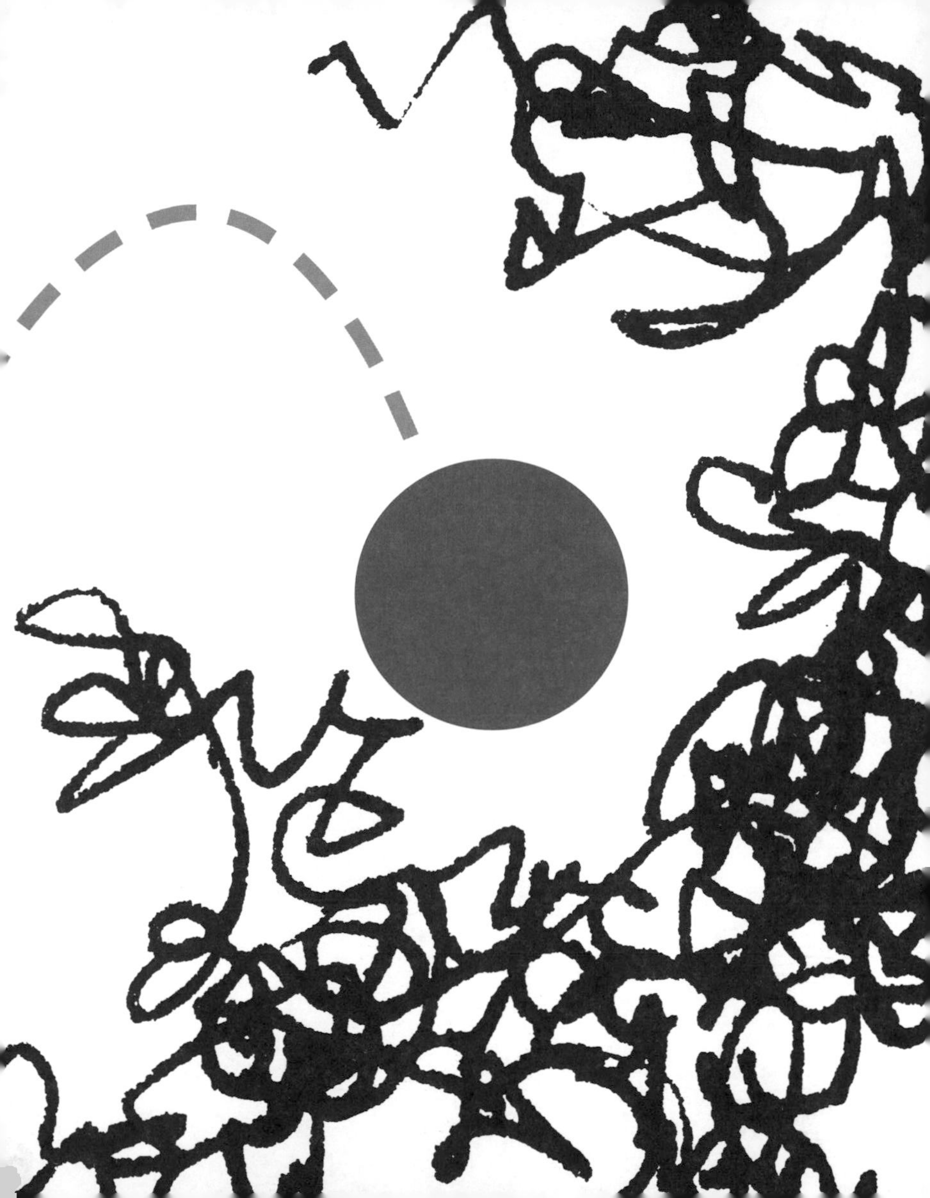

"and you are as stiff as a stick.
Dull. Conventional and repressed.
Tied and trammeled.
Subdued, smothered and stifled.
Squashed, squelched and quenched."

"Come around when you get straightened out, kid," the squiggle added with a rasping chuckle, as he chased her into the high grass.

"Why take chances," replied the line without much conviction. "I'm dependable.

I know where I'm going.

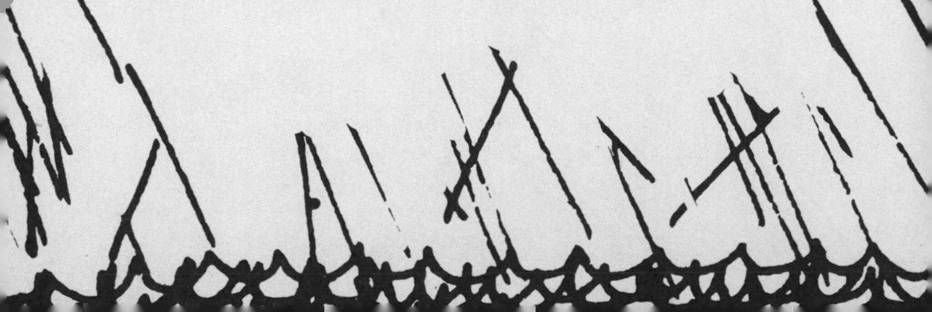

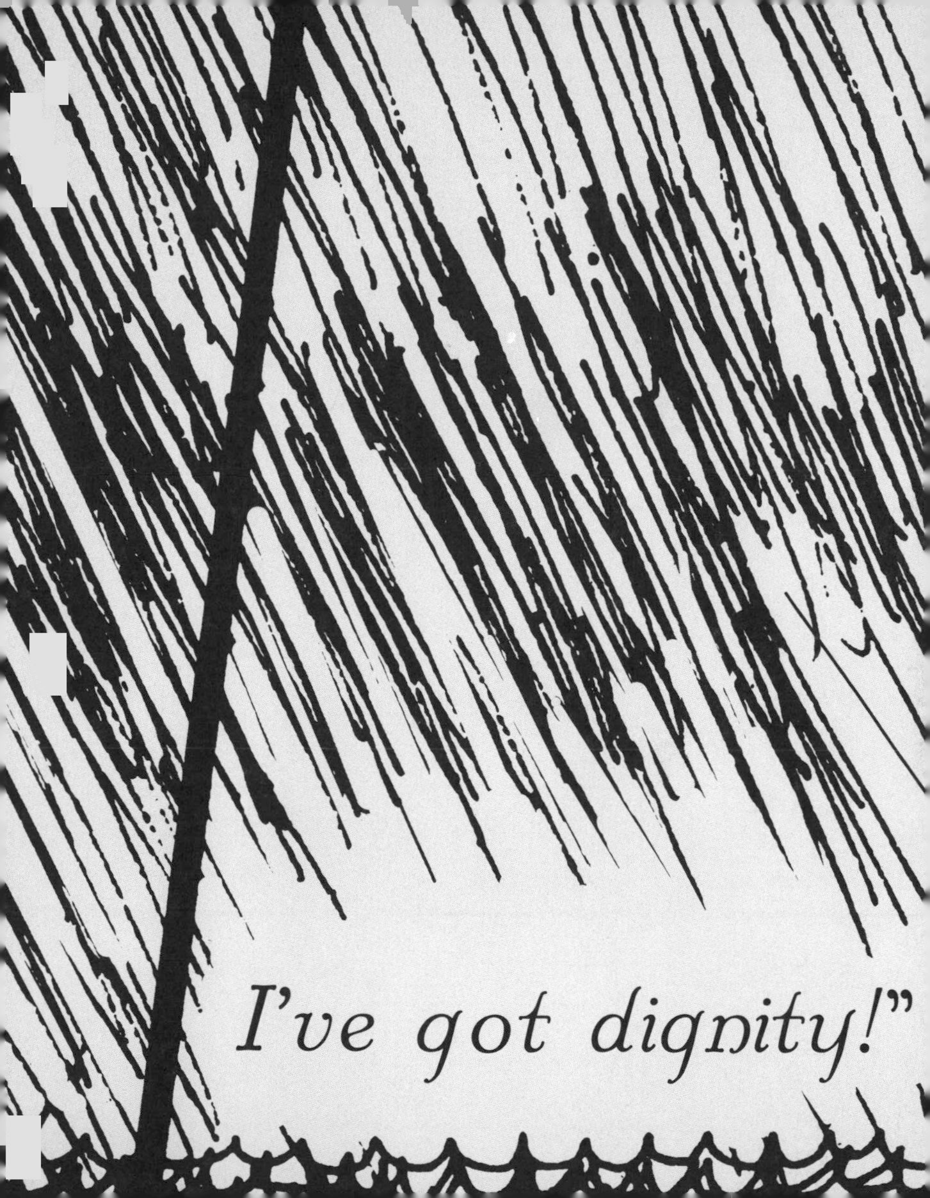

I've got dignity!"

But this was small consolation for the miserable line.

Each day

he grew

more

and

more

morose.

He stopped

eating

or sleeping

and before long was completely on edge.

*His worried friends noticed
how terribly thin and drawn
he had become and did their best
to cheer him up.*

"She's not good enough for you."

"She lacks depth."

*"They all look alike anyway.
Why don't you find a nice
straight line and settle down?"*

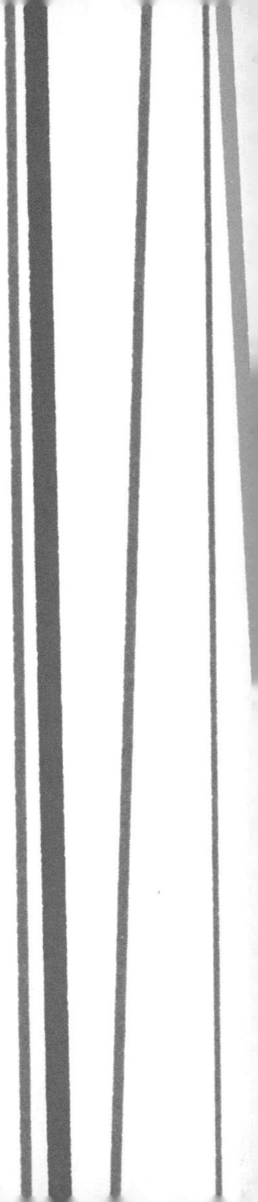

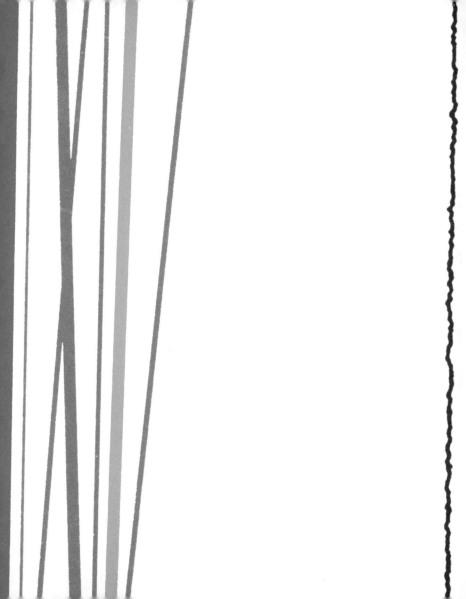

But he hardly heard a word they said.
Any way he looked at her she was perfect.

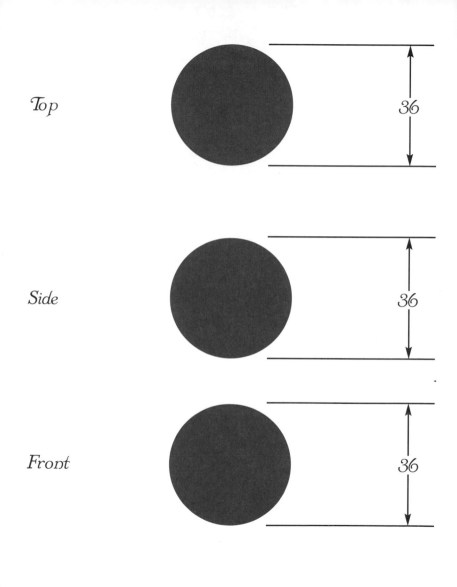

Top

36

Side

36

Front

36

He saw things in her that no one else
could possibly imagine.

"She is more beautiful than any straight line
I've ever seen," he sighed wistfully,
and they all shook their heads.
Even allowing for his feelings
they felt this was stretching a point.

And so he spent his time dreaming
of the inconstant dot and imagining himself
as the forceful figure she was sure to admire—

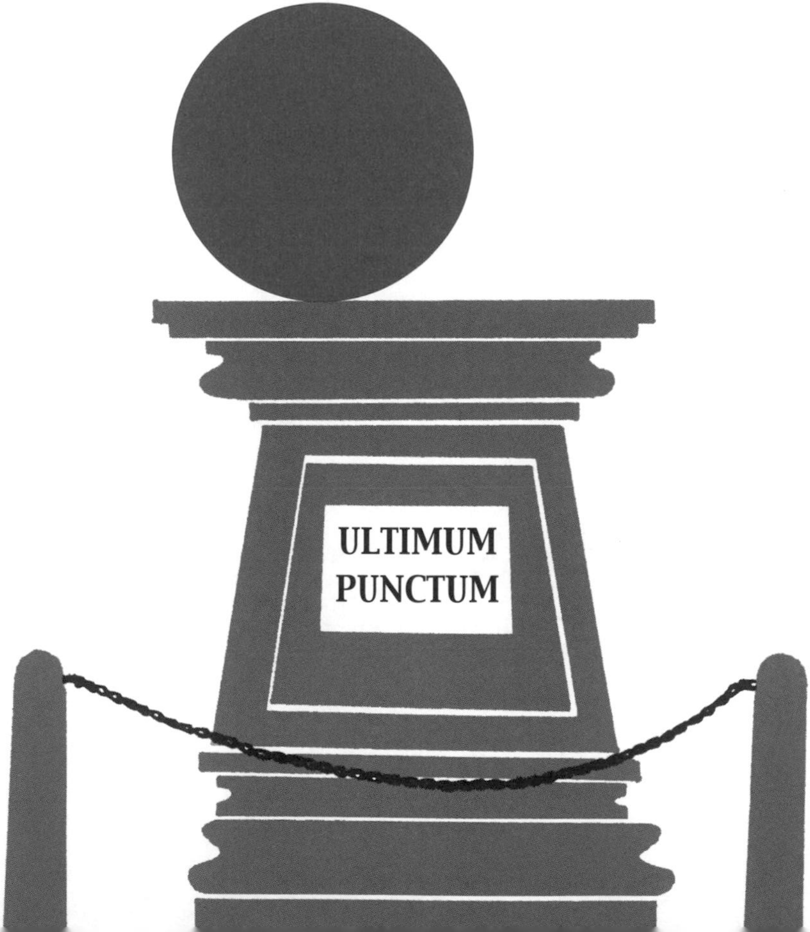
ULTIMUM
PUNCTUM

THE LINE AS A
CELEBRATED DAREDEVIL

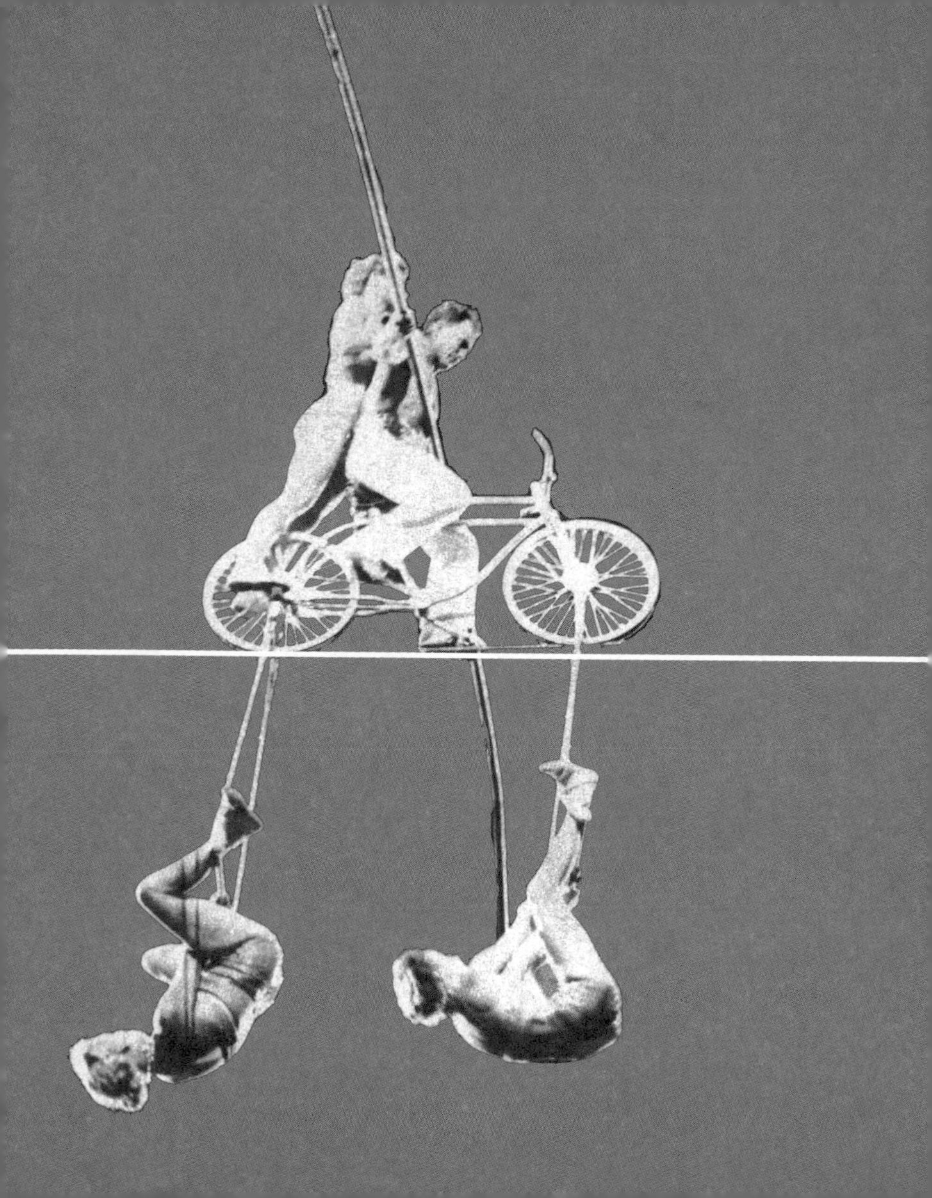

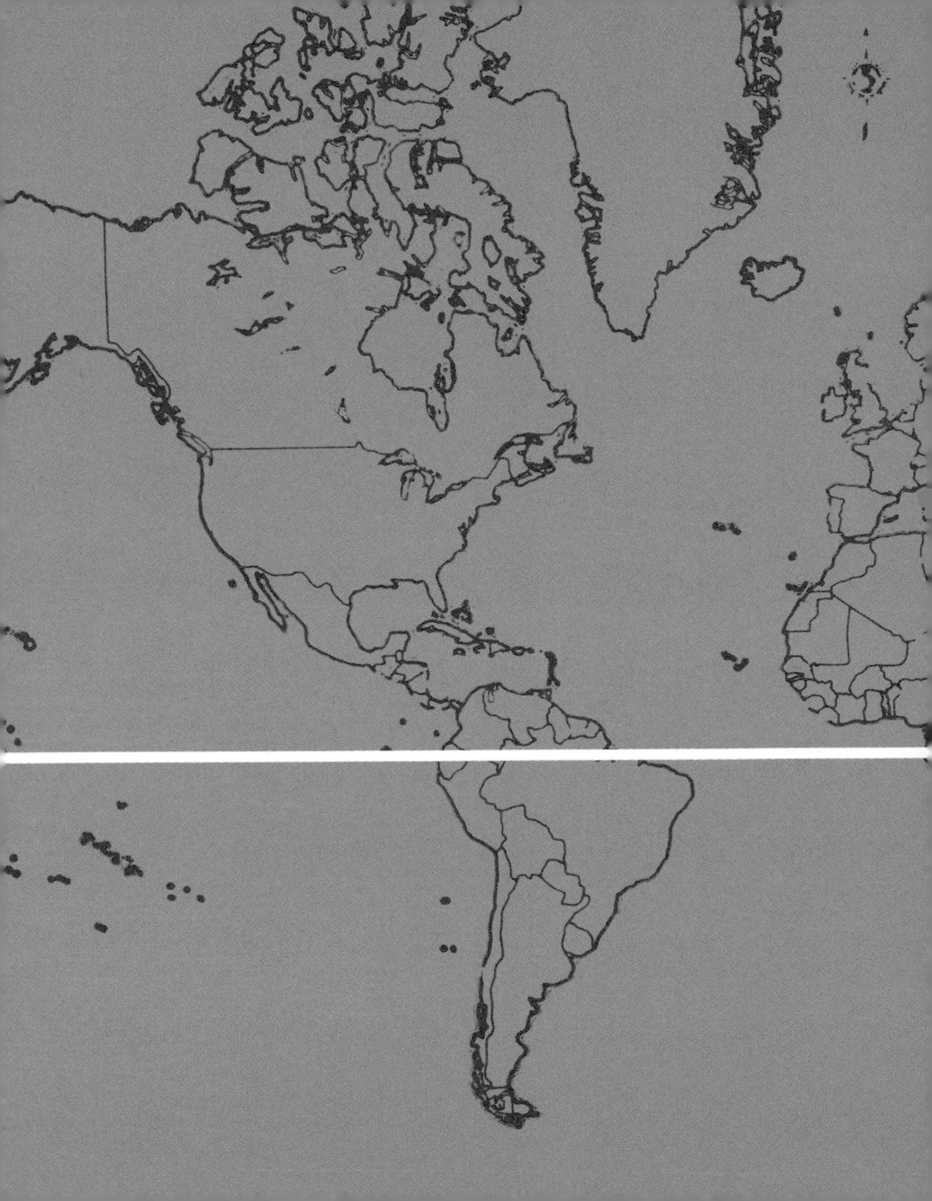

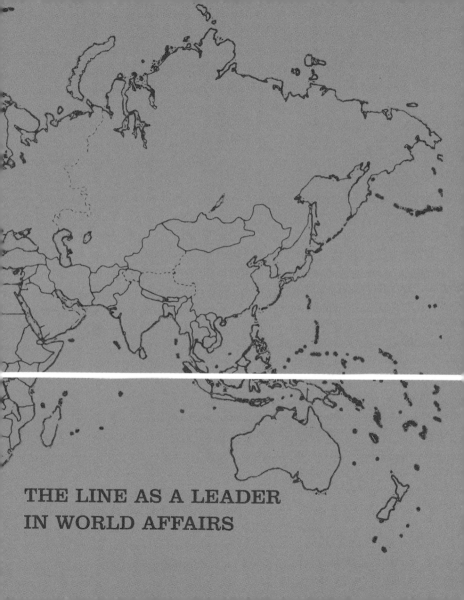

THE LINE AS A LEADER
IN WORLD AFFAIRS

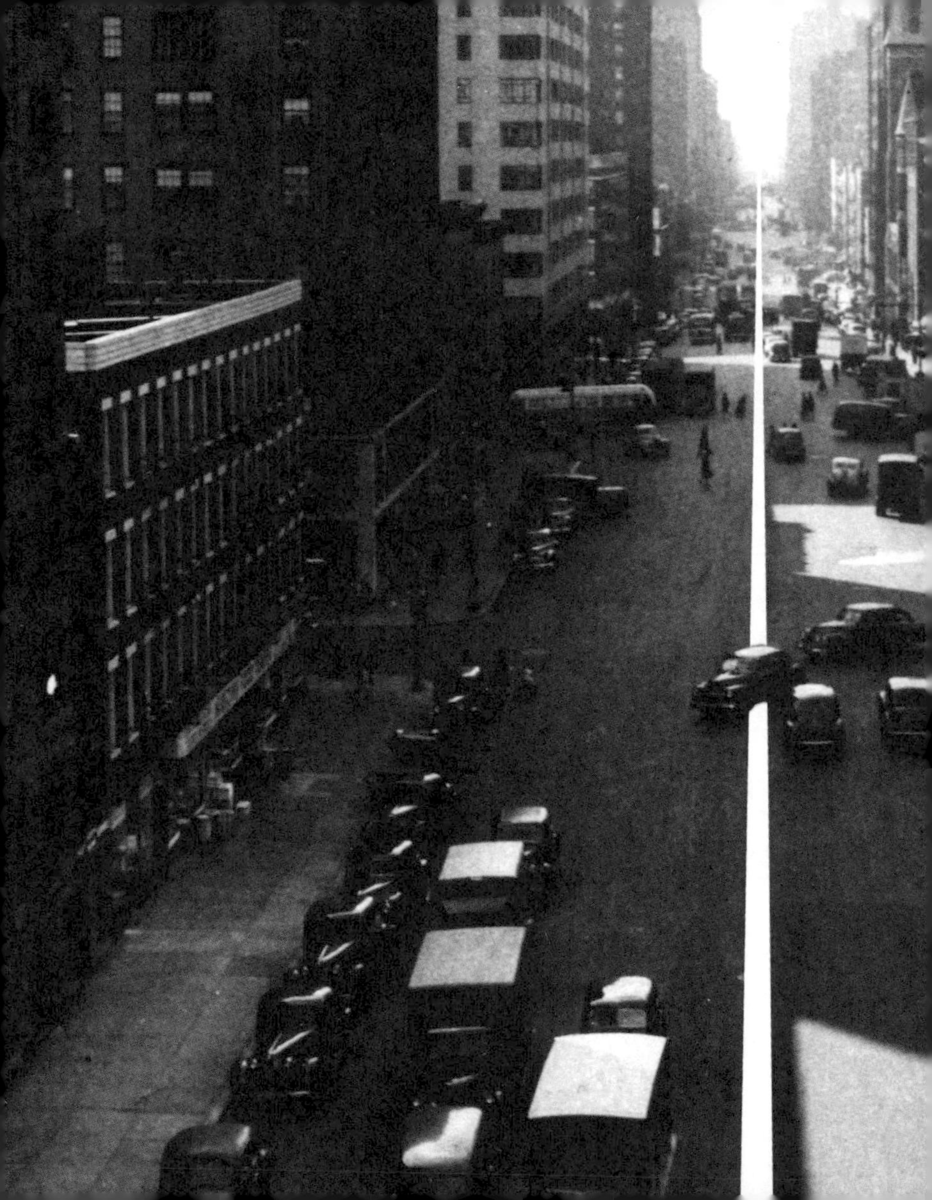

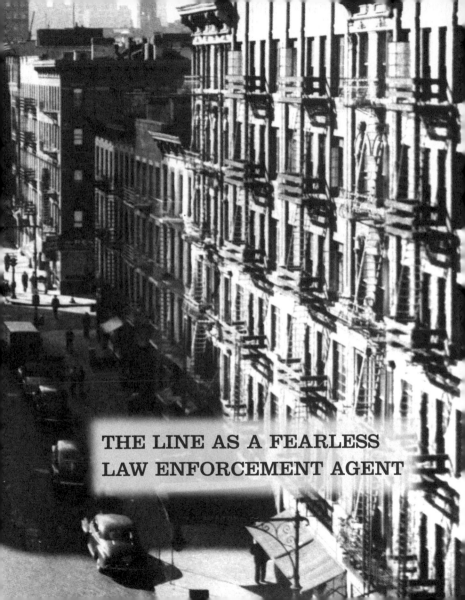

THE LINE AS A FEARLESS
LAW ENFORCEMENT AGENT

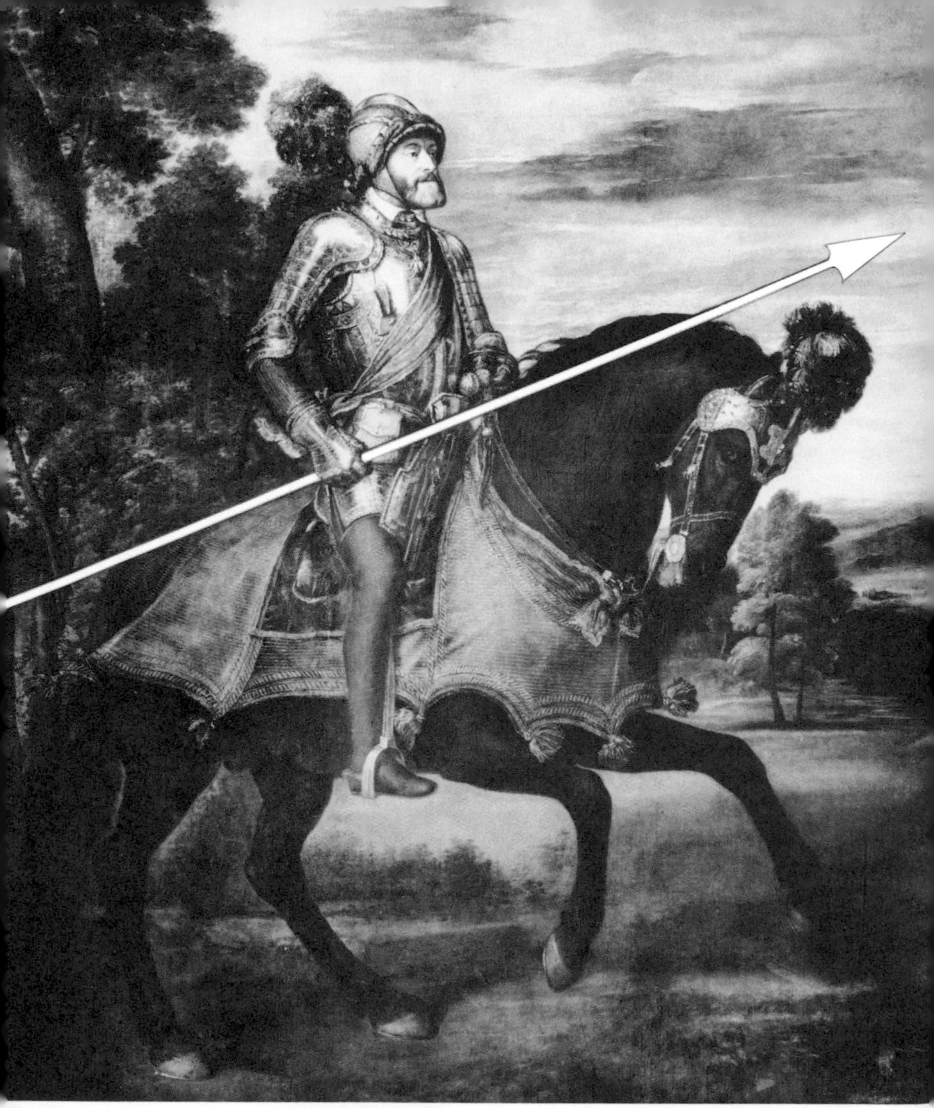

THE LINE AS A POTENT FORCE

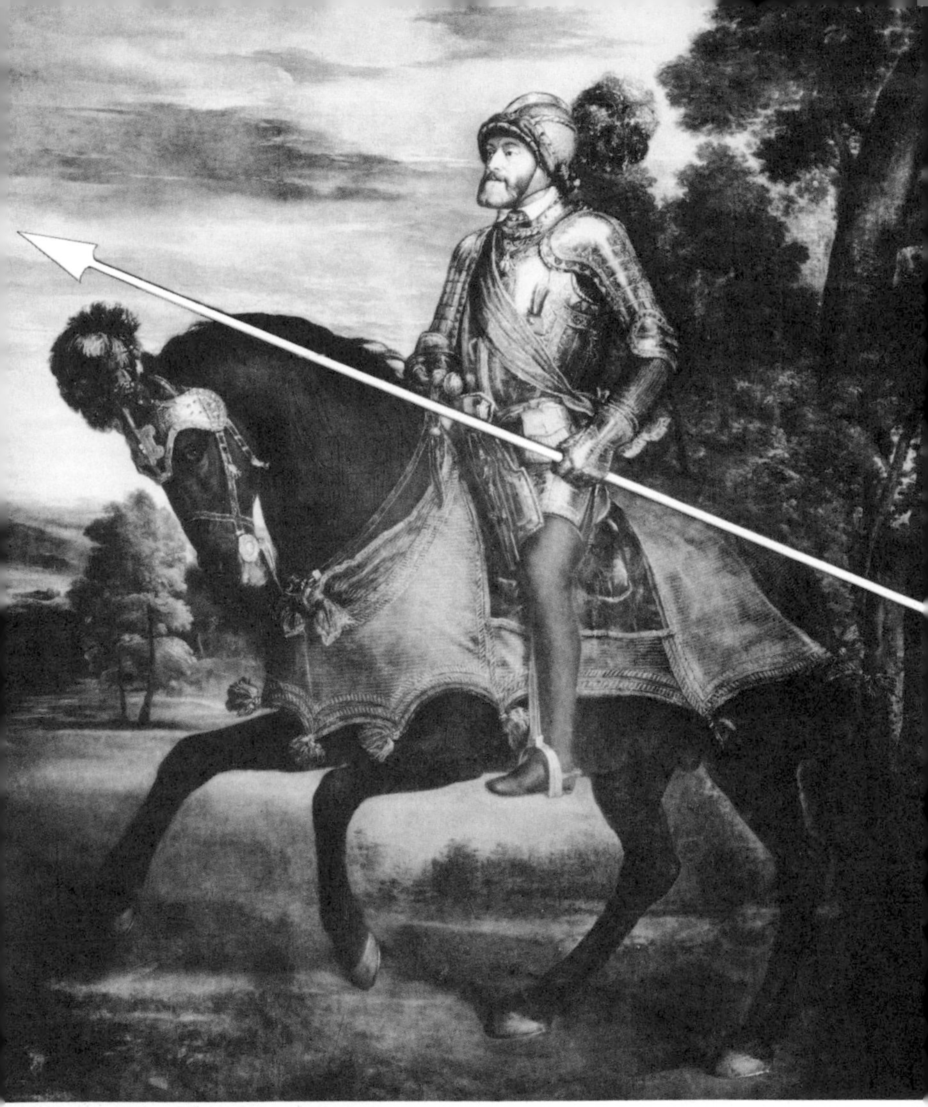

IN THE WORLD OF ART

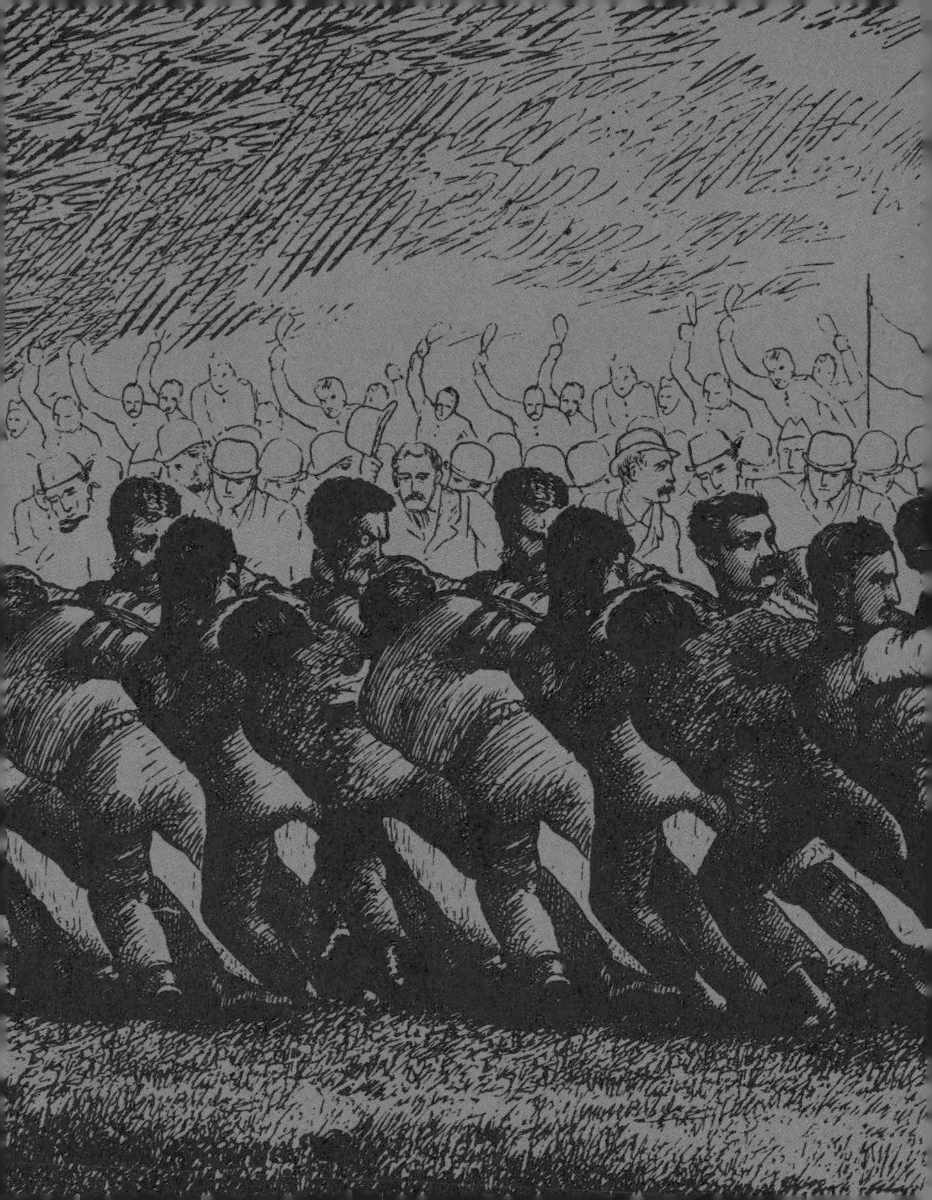

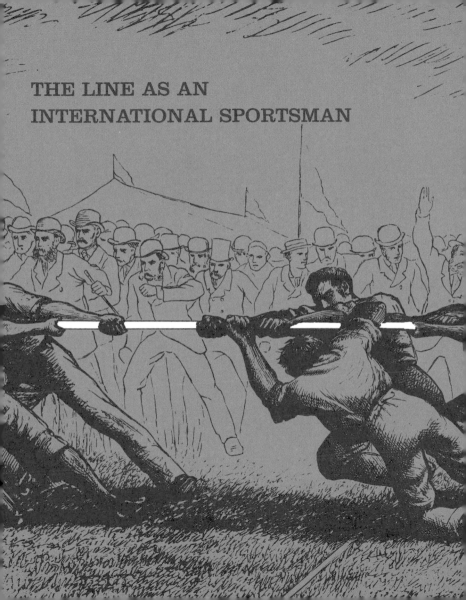

THE LINE AS AN INTERNATIONAL SPORTSMAN

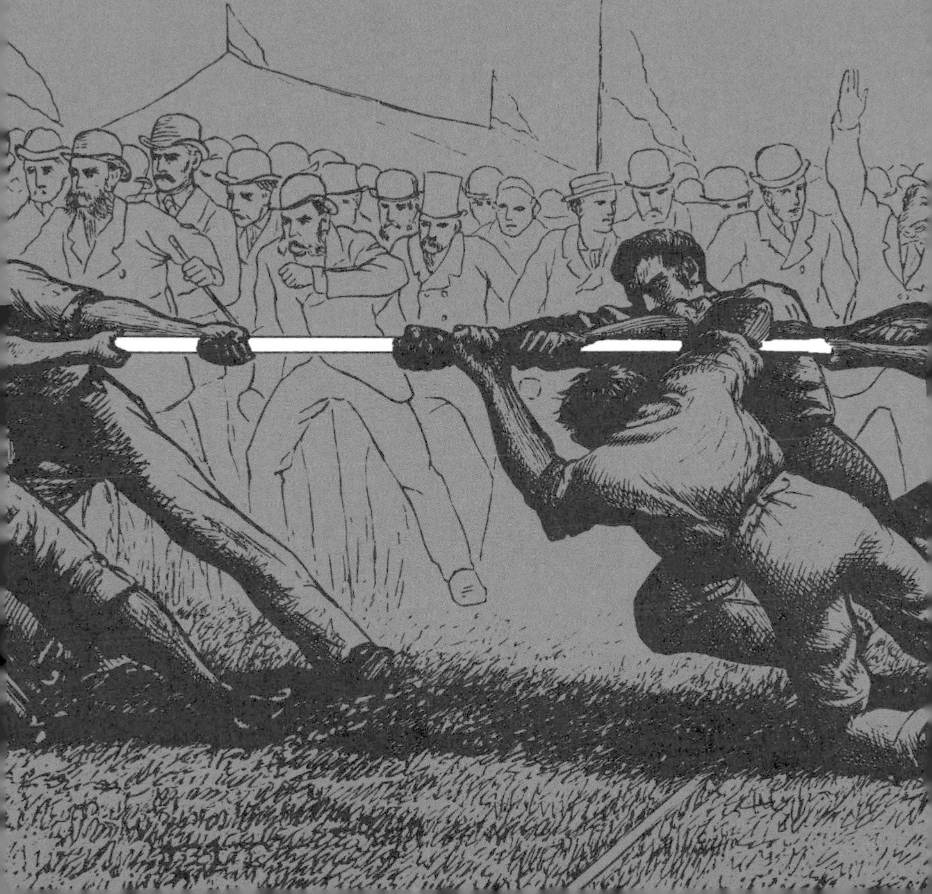

But he soon grew tired of self-deception and decided that perhaps the squiggly line might have the answer after all.

"I lack spontaneity. I must learn to let go, to be free, to express the inner passionate me."

But it just didn't make any difference, for no matter how often, or how hard he tried,

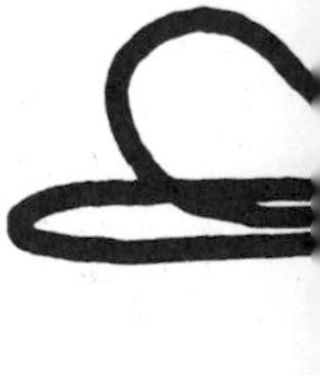

he always ended up the same way.

And yet he continued trying
and failing and trying again.
Until when he had all but given up,
he discovered at last that with
great concentration and self-control
he was able to change direction
and bend wherever he chose.

So he did, and made an angle.

And then again and made another

and then another and then another and then another and then another and then another

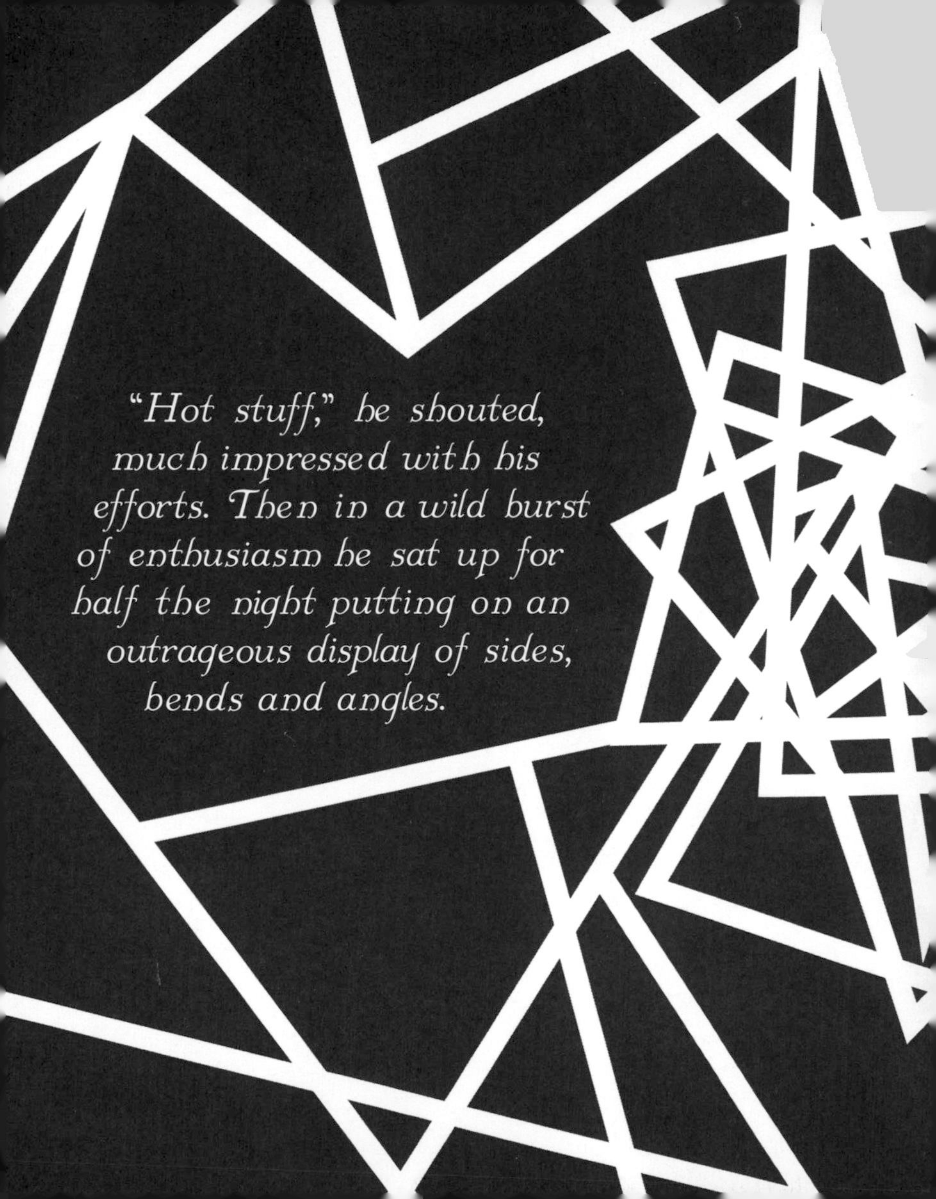

"Hot stuff," he shouted, much impressed with his efforts. Then in a wild burst of enthusiasm he sat up for half the night putting on an outrageous display of sides, bends and angles.

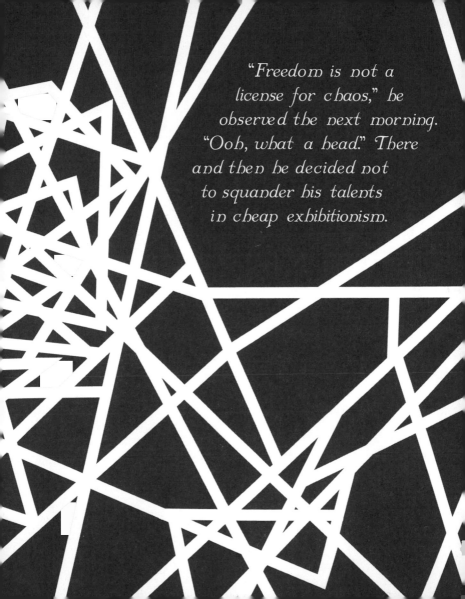

"Freedom is not a license for chaos," he observed the next morning. "Ooh, what a head." There and then he decided not to squander his talents in cheap exhibitionism.

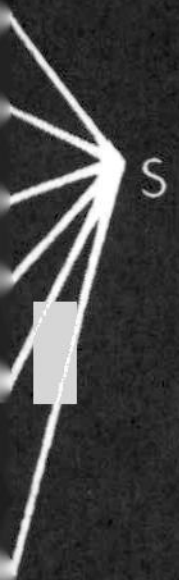
S

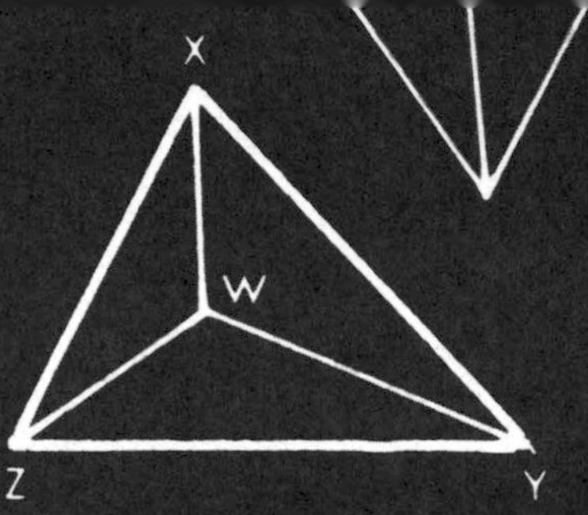
X
W
Z
Y

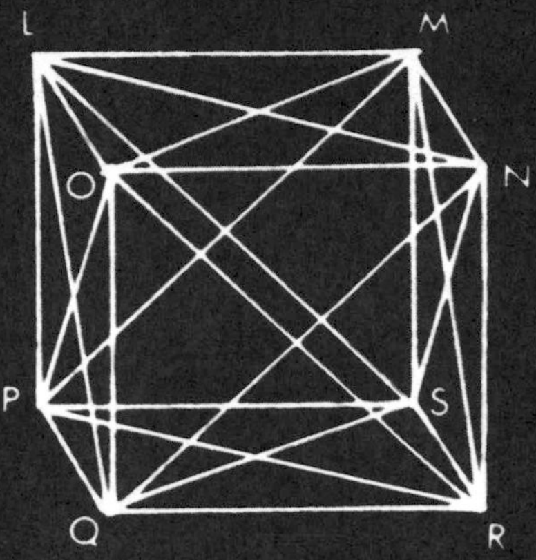
L
M
O
N
P
S
Q
R

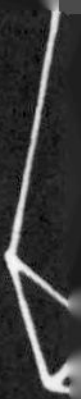

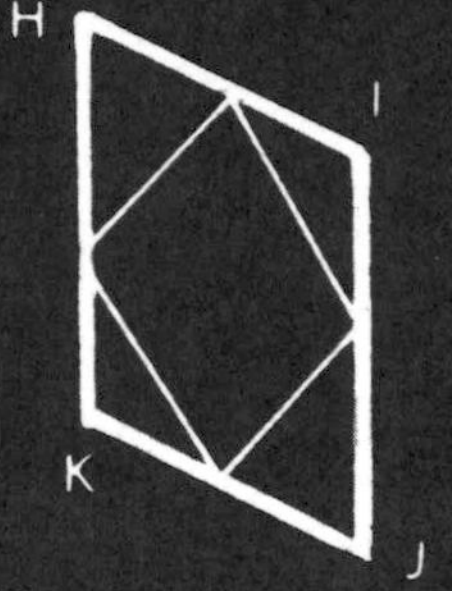
H
I
K
J

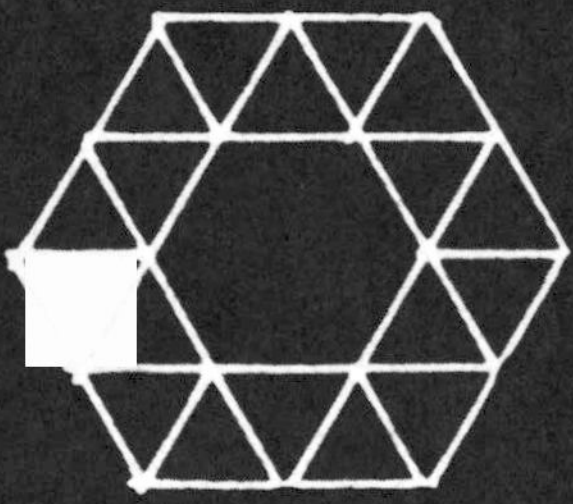

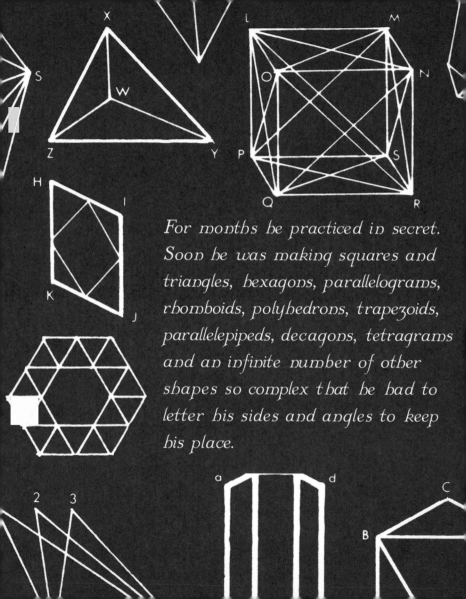

For months he practiced in secret. Soon he was making squares and triangles, hexagons, parallelograms, rhomboids, polyhedrons, trapezoids, parallelepipeds, decagons, tetragrams and an infinite number of other shapes so complex that he had to letter his sides and angles to keep his place.

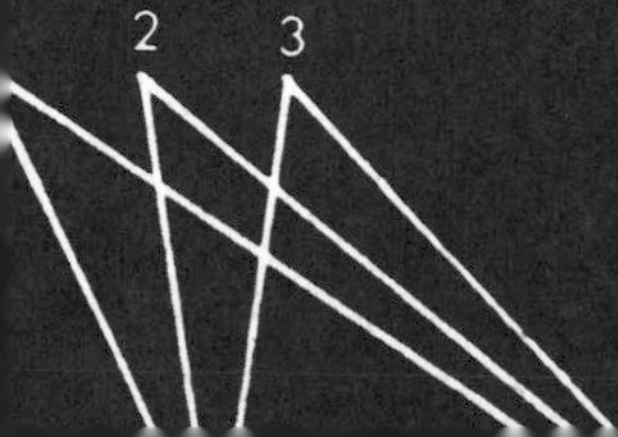
2
3

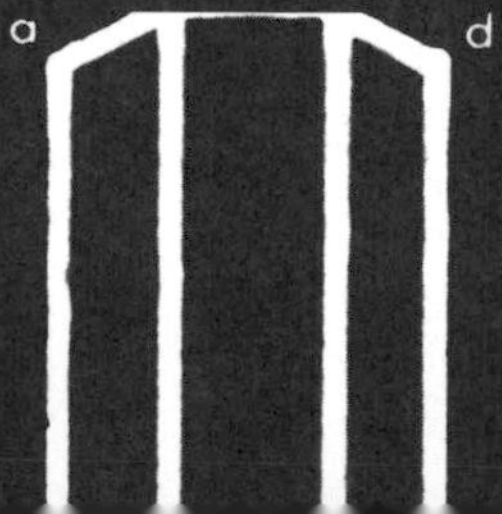
a
d

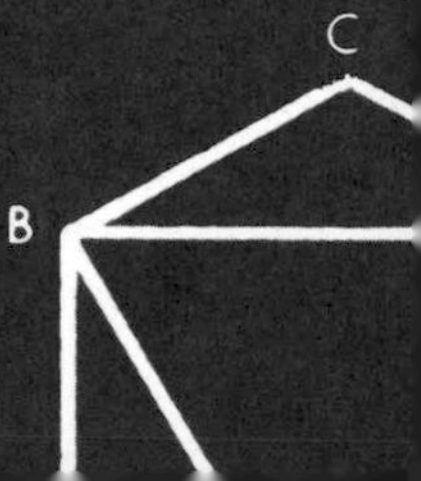
C
B

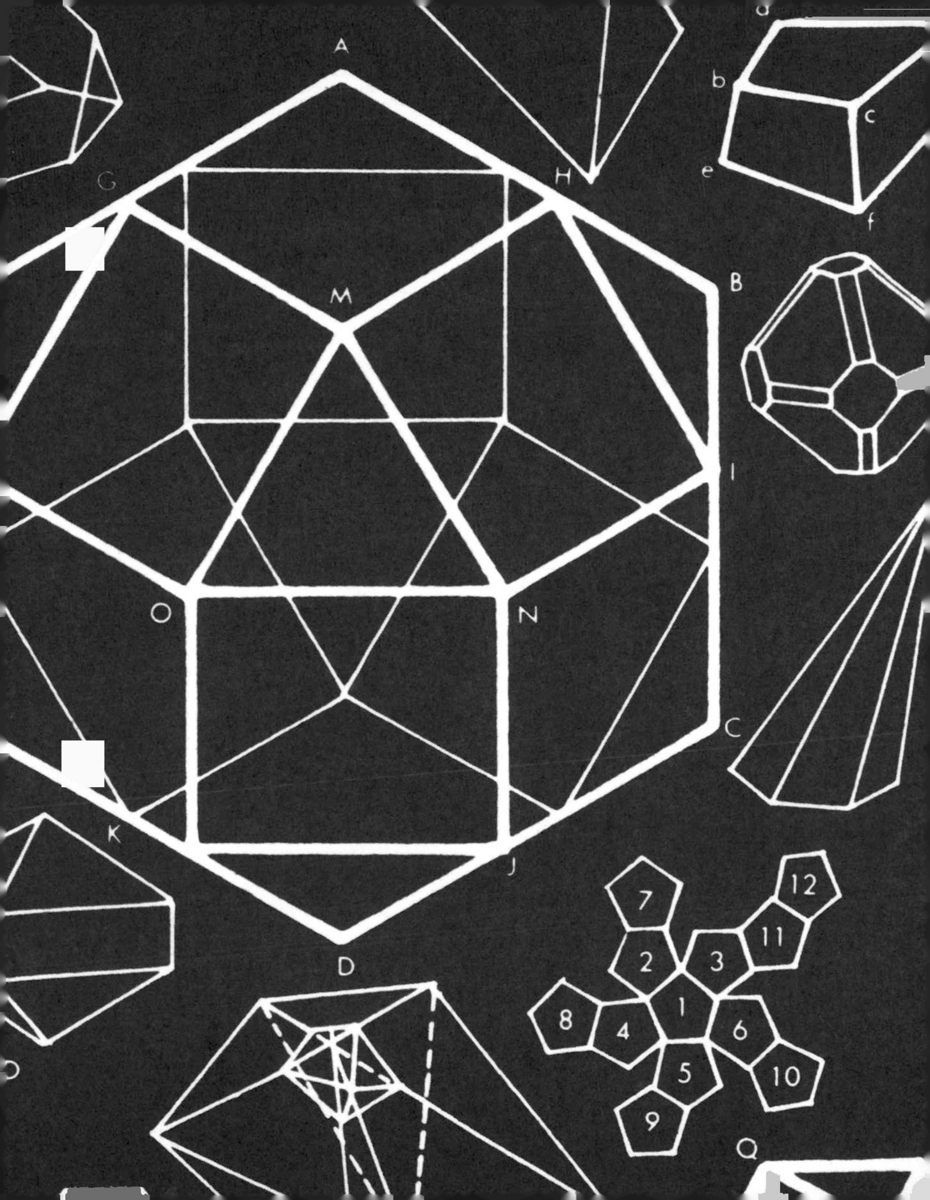
A
G
H
b
c
e
f
B
M
I
O
N
C
K
J
D
7
12
2
3
11
1
8
4
6
5
10
9
Q

Before long he had learned to carefully control ellipses, circles and complex curves

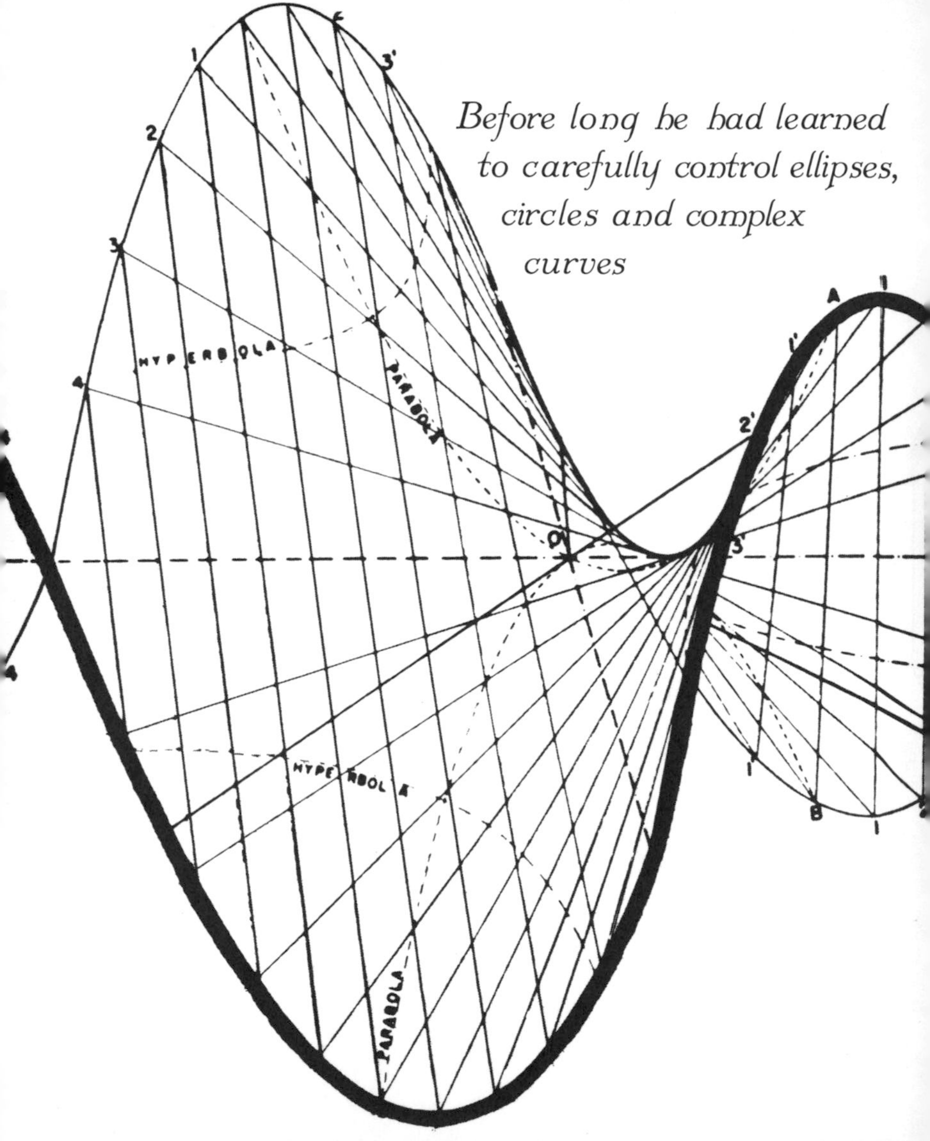
HYPERBOLA
PARABOLA
HYPERBOLA
PARABOLA

and to express himself in any shape he wished–

"You name it, I'll play it."

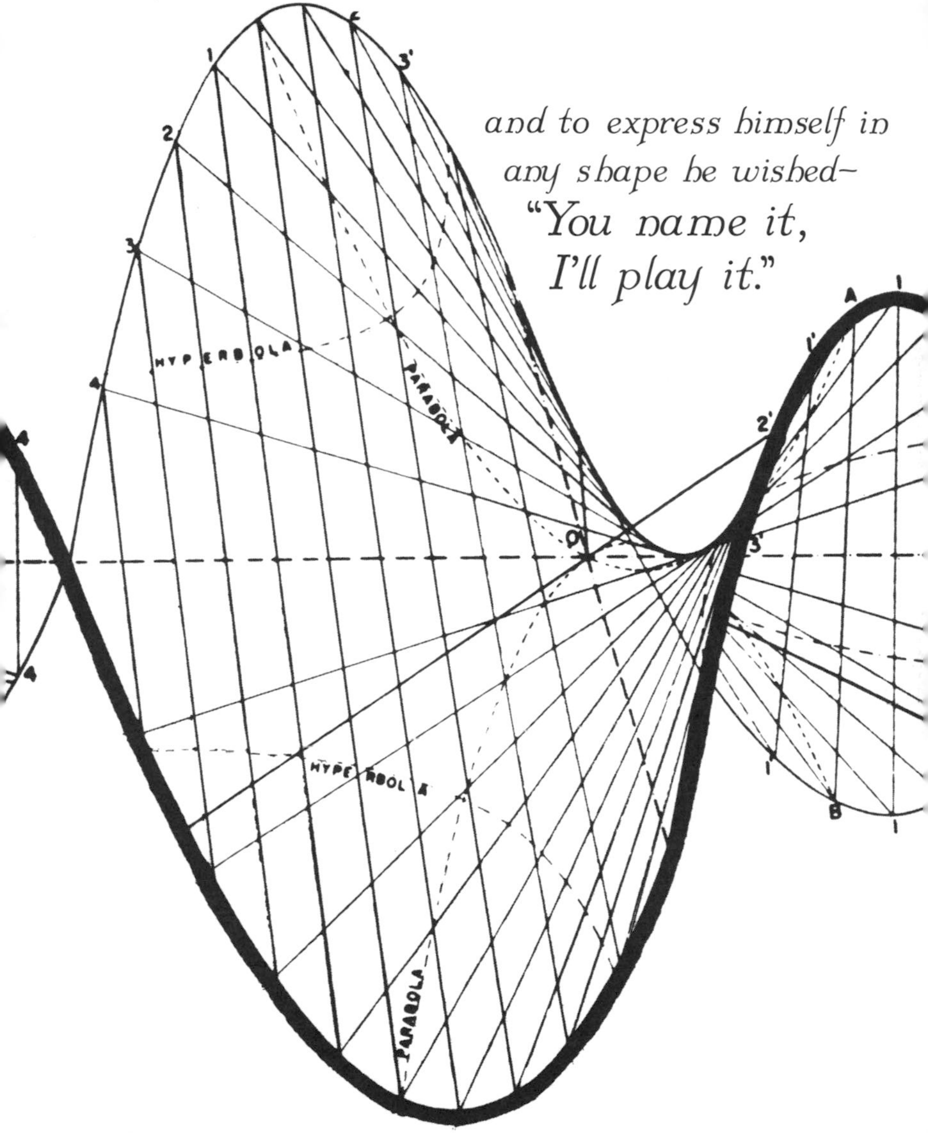
HYPERBOLA
PARABOLA
HYPERBOLA
PARABOLA
O
A
B

But all his successes meant nothing to him alone and so off he went to seek the dot once again.

"He doesn't stand a chance," muttered the squiggle in a voice that sounded like bad plumbing.

But the line, who was bursting with old love and new confidence, was not to be denied. Throughout the evening he was by turns–

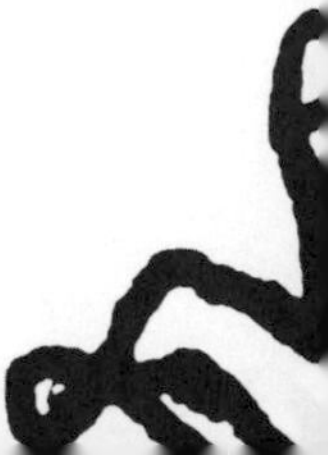

MYSTERIOUS

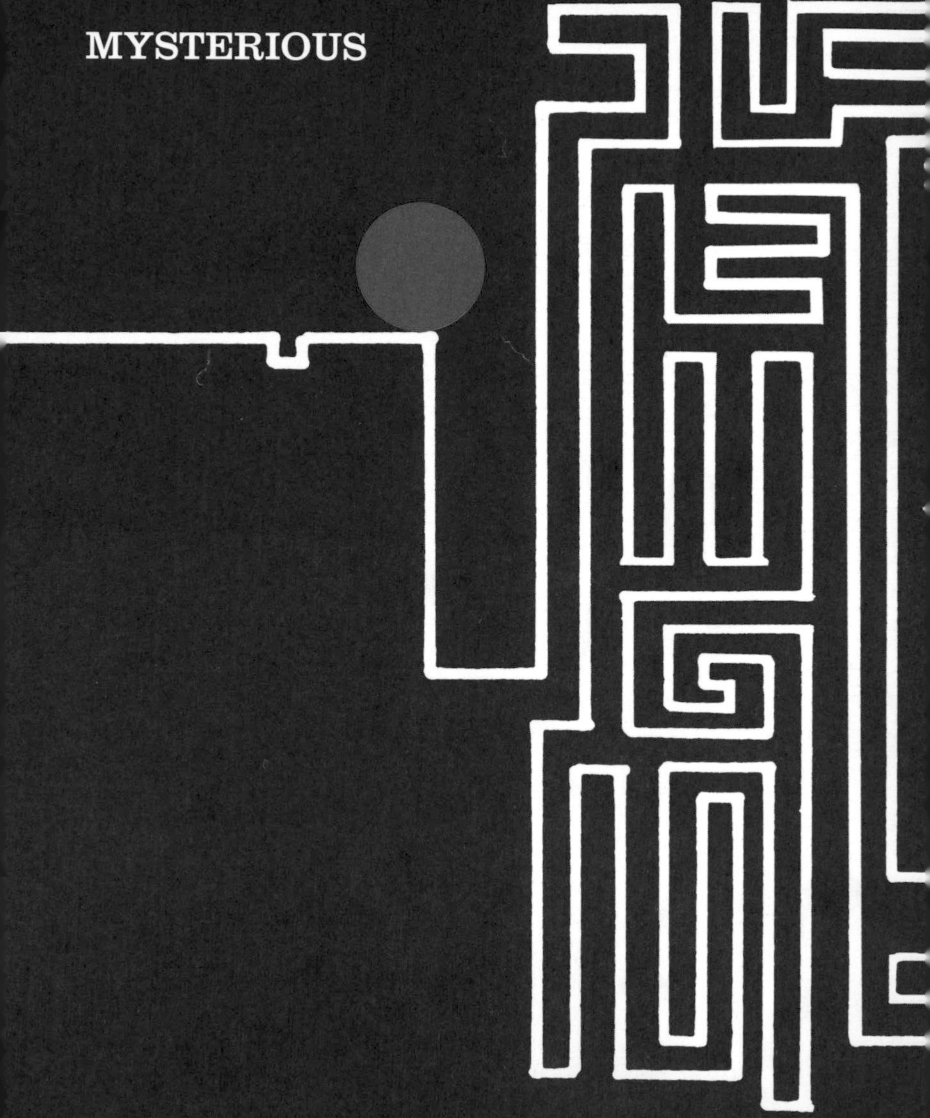

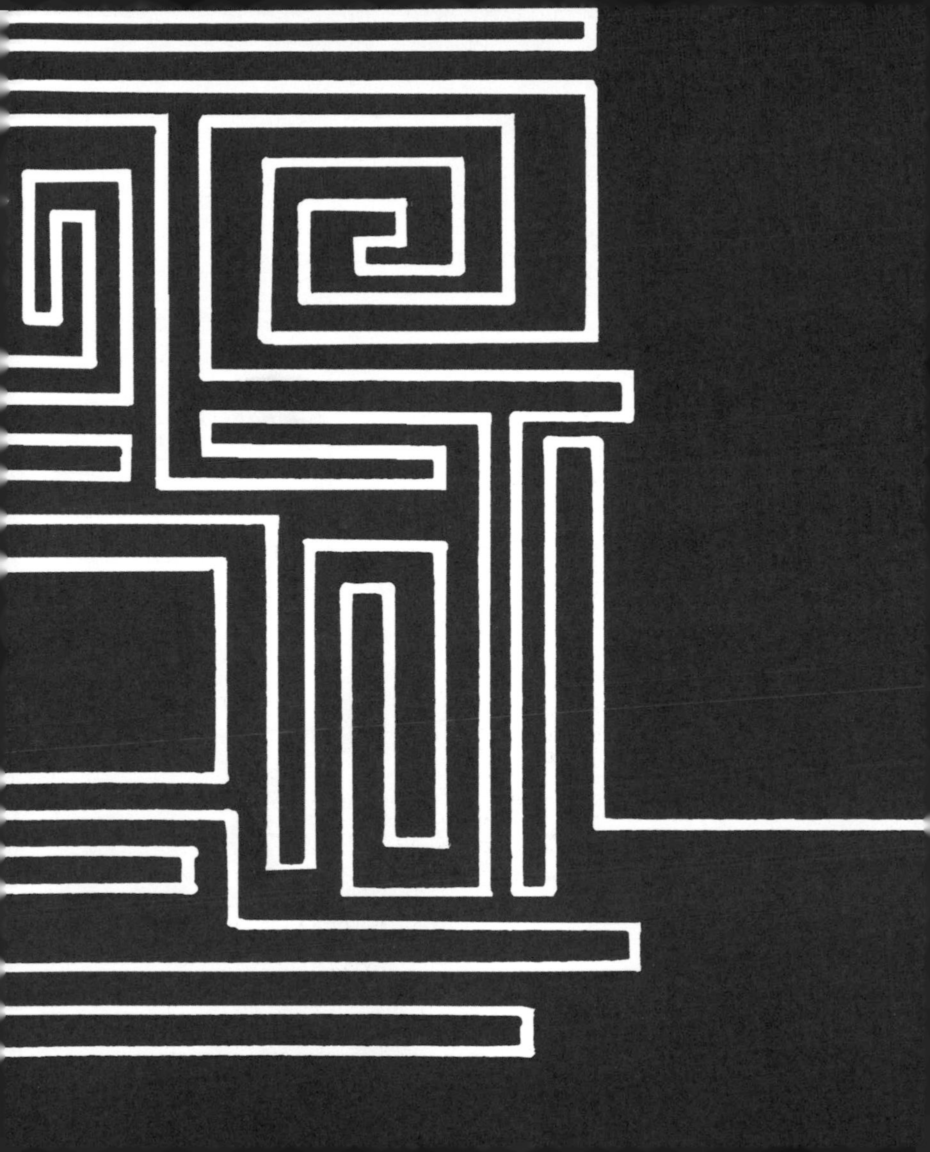

CLEVER

DAZZLING

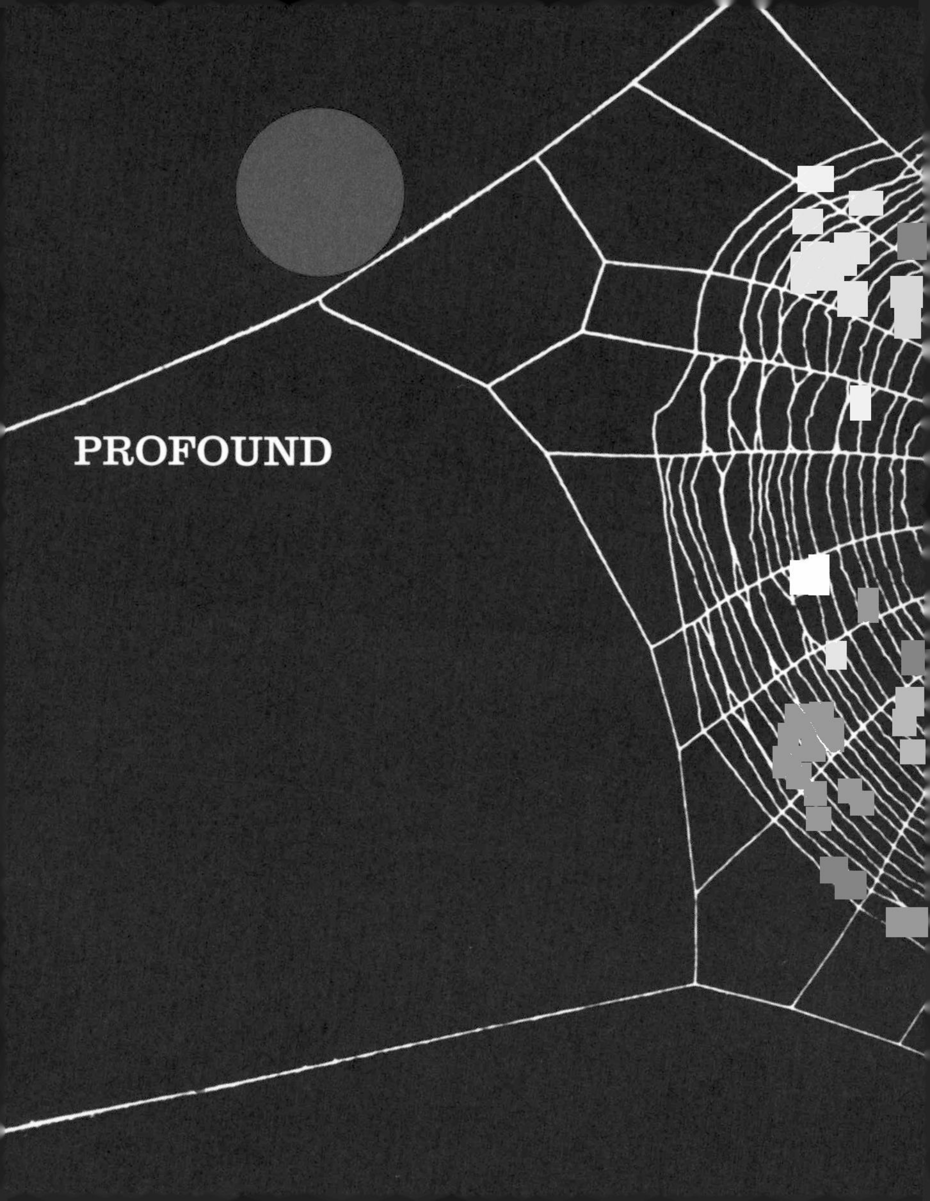
PROFOUND

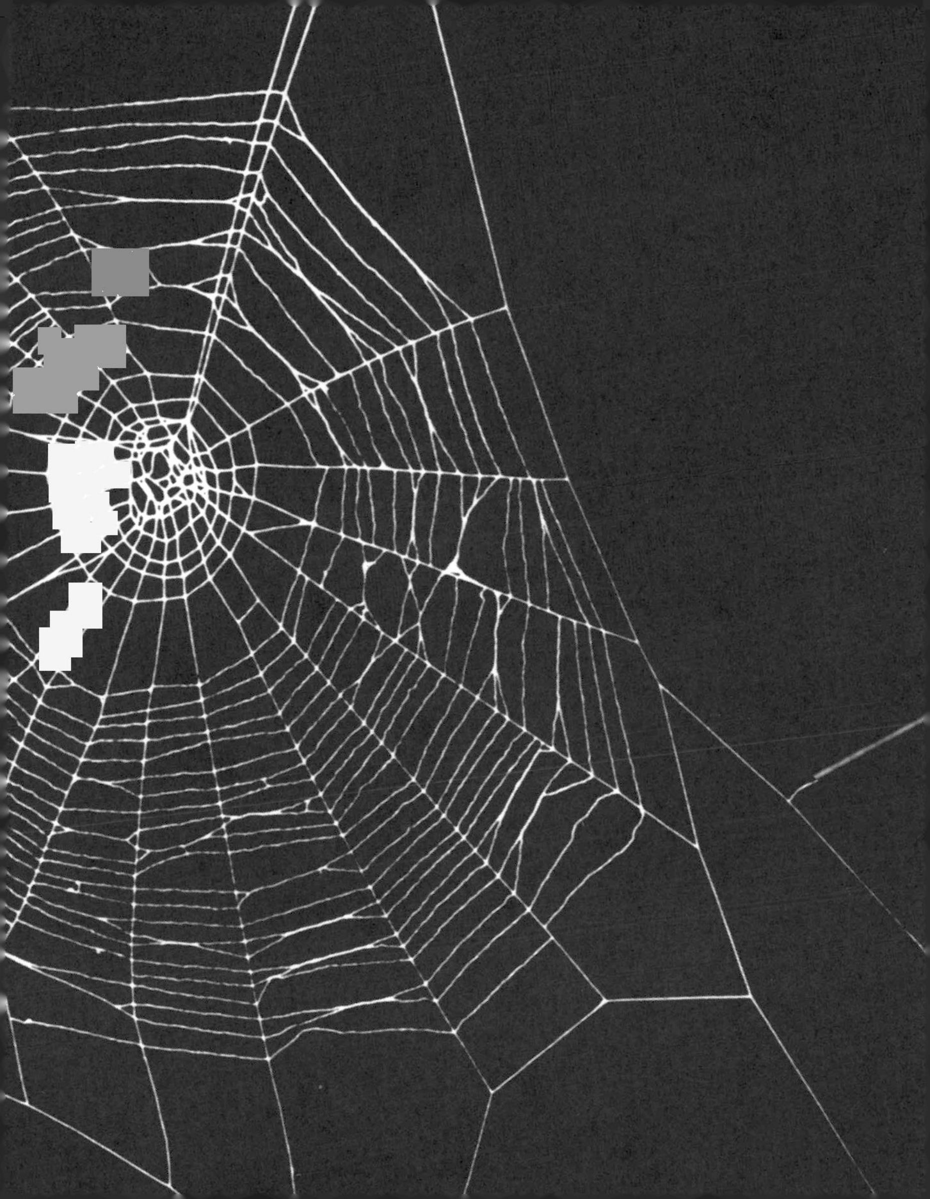

COMPLEX

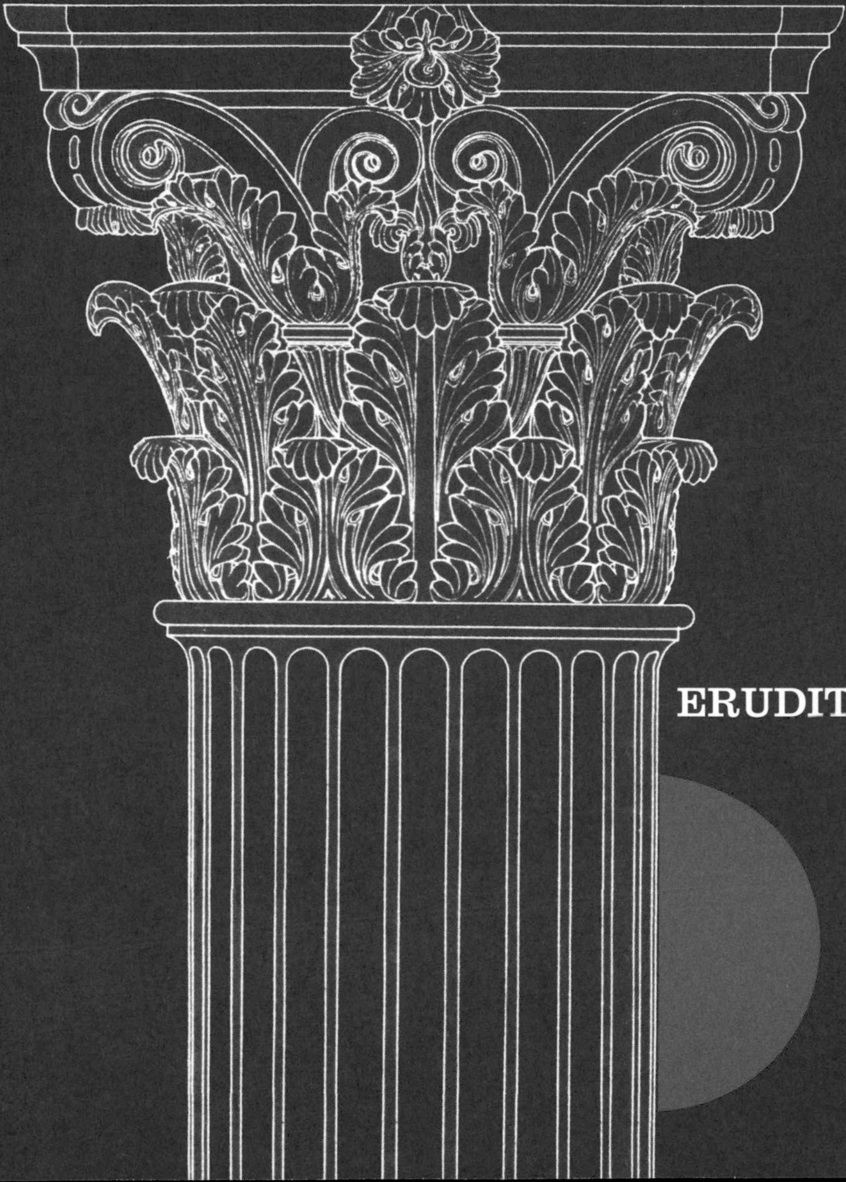

ERUDITE

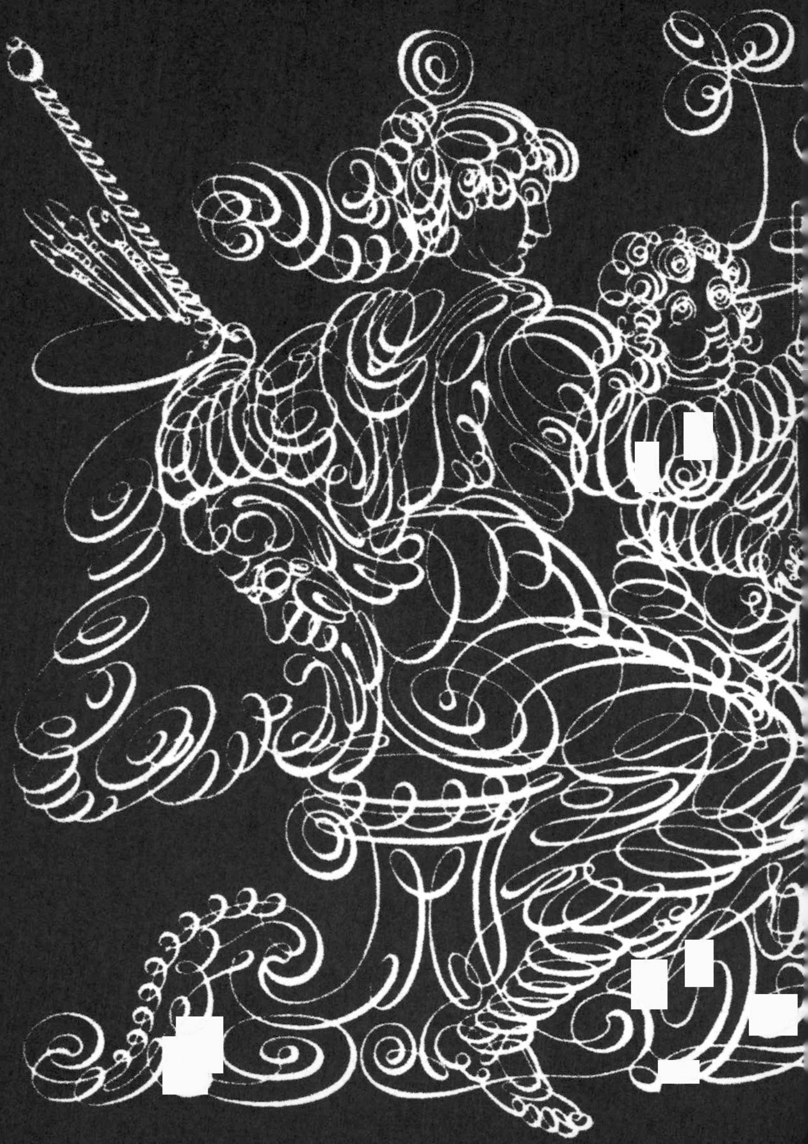

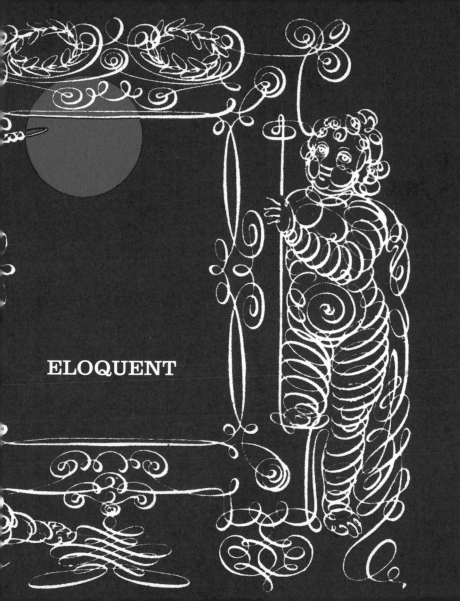

ELOQUENT

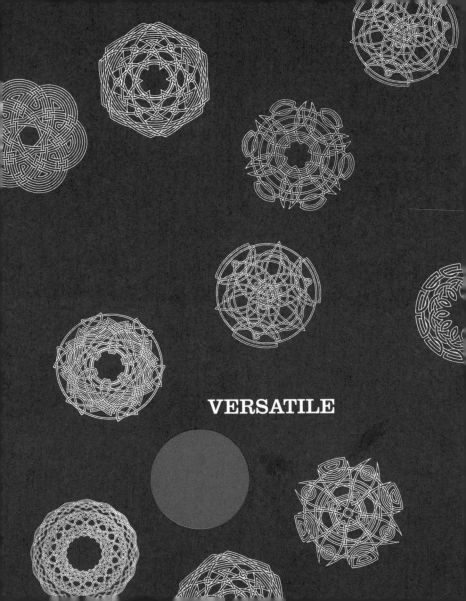

VERSATILE

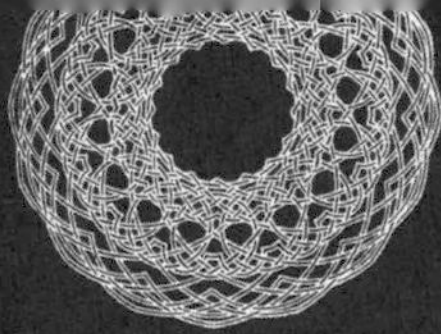

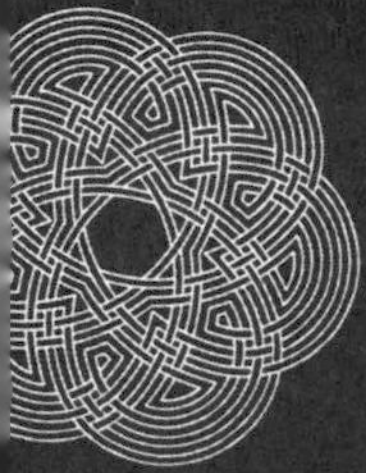

ENIGMATIC

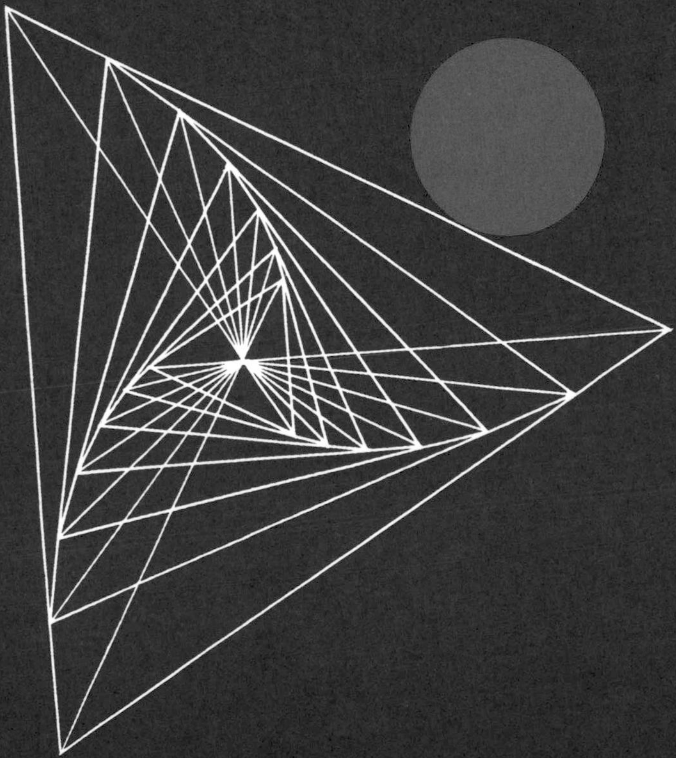

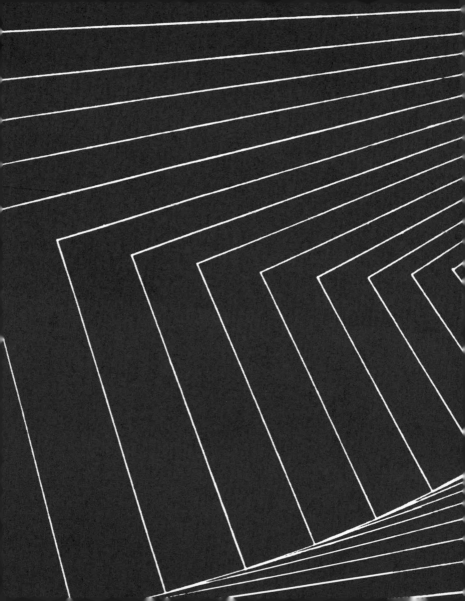

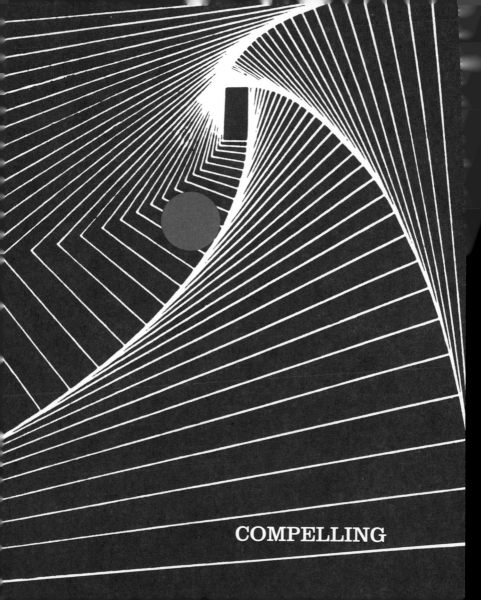

COMPELLING

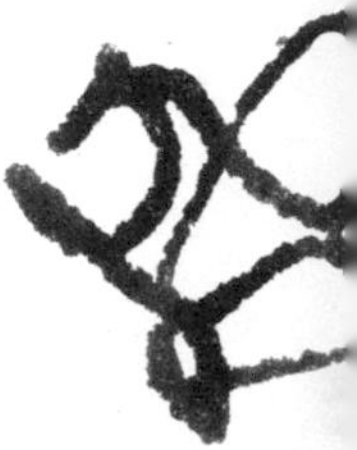

The dot was overwhelmed.
She giggled like a schoolgirl
and didn't know what to do with her hands.
Then she turned slowly to the squiggle,
who had suddenly developed a severe cramp.

"Well?" she inquired,
trying to give him every chance.

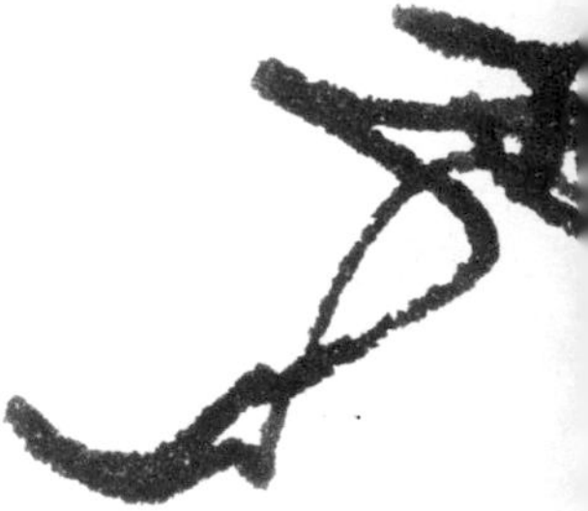

The squiggle, taken by surprise,
did the best he could.

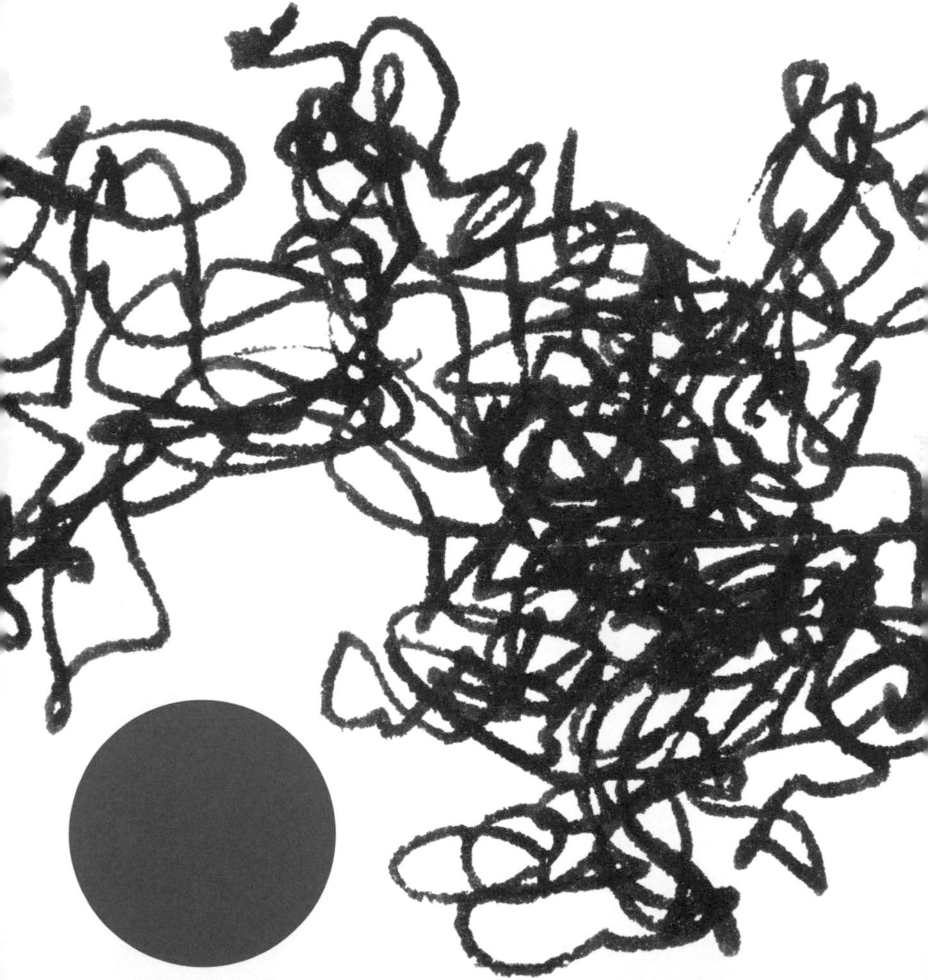

"Is that all?" she demanded.

"I guess so," replied the miserable squiggle. "That is, I suppose so. What I mean is I never know how it's going to turn out. Hey, have you heard the one about the two guys who—"

The dot wondered why she had never noticed how hairy and coarse he was, and how untidy and graceless, and how he mispronounced his L's and picked his ear.

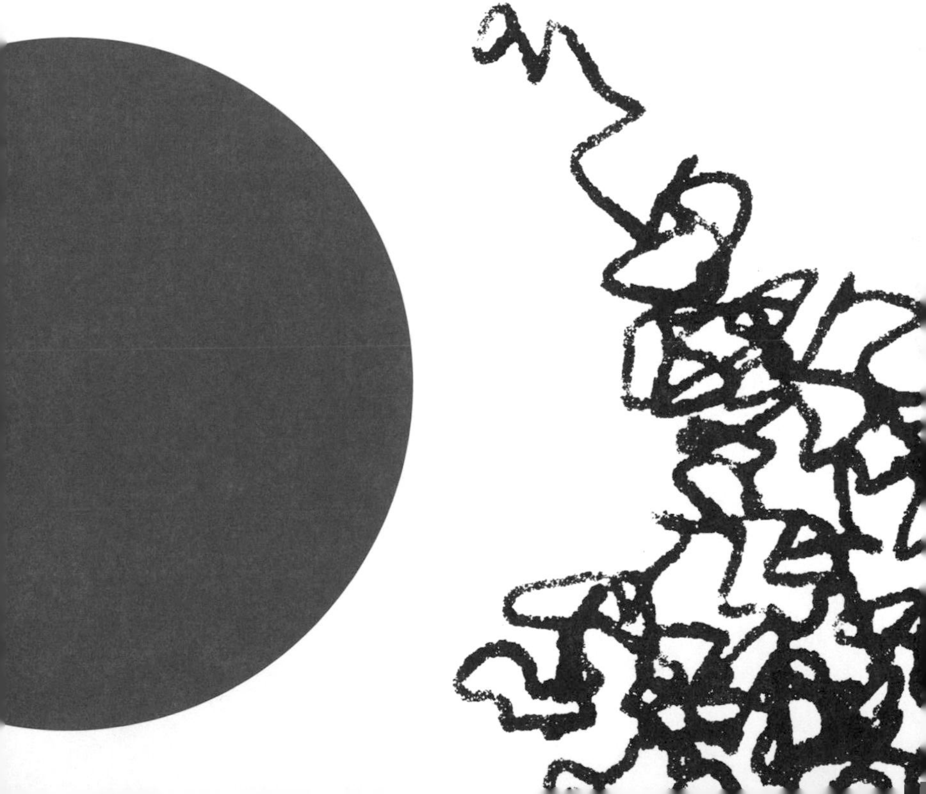

And suddenly she realized that what she had thought was freedom and joy was nothing but anarchy and sloth.

"You are as meaningless as a melon," she said coldly. "Undisciplined, unkempt and unaccountable, insignificant, indeterminate and inadvertent, out of shape, out of order, out of place and out of luck."

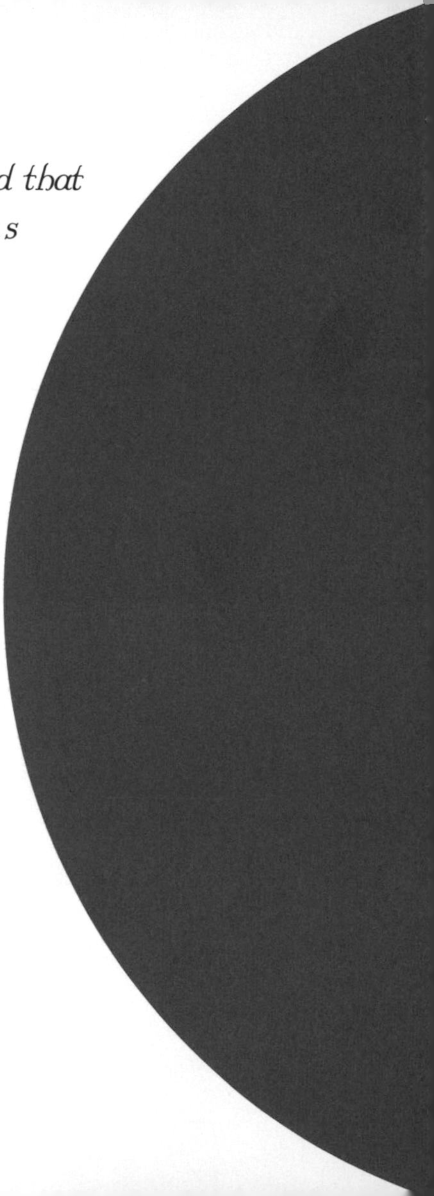